THE MYSTERY OF THE
SINGING SERPENT

The Three Investigators peered
into the chamber from their
hiding place behind the door.
Twelve people were sitting at the
large, round table in the middle of
the room.

Everyone was still.

Suddenly they heard a shrill
sound. Someone—or something—
was singing.

The boys trembled.

Then they saw the horrible
apparition. It was a huge cobra, a
shimmer of green and blue, a
spread of hood, a red-eyed glitter.
The thing was deadly—in more
ways than one!

ALFRED HITCHCOCK
and The Three Investigators in

THE MYSTERY OF THE SINGING SERPENT

Text by M. V. Carey

Based on characters created by Robert Arthur

 Random House · New York

The Mystery of the Singing Serpent

Originally published by Random House in 1972
First Random House paperback edition, 1981

Library of Congress Cataloging in Publication Data:

Carey, M   V
    Alfred Hitchcock and the three investigators in
The mystery of the singing serpent.

    ([Alfred Hitchcock and the three investigators]   ;   17)

    SUMMARY: The Three Investigators become involved in witchcraft
when they try to rescue a woman from the influence of snake worshipers.

    [1.   Mystery and detective stories.   2.   Witchcraft—Fiction]
I.   Arthur, Robert.   II.   Title.   III.   Title: Mystery of the singing serpent.
IV.   Series.

[PZ7. C213Alb   1981]   [Fic]   80-18947
ISBN 0-394-84678-8 (pbk.)

Also available in Gibraltar Library Binding

Manufactured in the United States of America
1   2   3   4   5   6   7   8   9   0

Contents

A Short Preview
by Alfred Hitchcock

Welcome, mystery lovers! We are gathered together again for another stimulating case of The Three Investigators, whose official motto is "We Investigate Anything." If they had known what they were getting into when they tackled the curious case of the singing serpent, they might have changed their motto!

Be that as it may, they find themselves this time drawn into the dark world of witchcraft, where mystery and intrigue lead them from one enigma to another until—but I am not a blabbermouth. I promised faithfully not to tell too much, and I shall keep my promise.

Indeed, I shall only say that The Three Investigators are Jupiter Jones, Pete Crenshaw and Bob Andrews, who all make their home in Rocky Beach, a small municipality in California a few miles from Hollywood. Their Headquarters is a mobile home trailer in The Jones Salvage Yard, a super-junkyard owned by Jupiter's aunt and uncle.

The boys make an excellent team. Jupiter has a quick mind and is adept at deductions. Pete is less intellectual but sturdy and courageous. Bob is somewhat studious and an excellent researcher. Together they have solved some very unusual mysteries indeed.

Which is all I shall say at this time, for I know you are eager to dispense with this preview and get to the main feature!

Alfred Hitchcock

THE MYSTERY OF THE
SINGING SERPENT

The Girl on the Appaloosa

1

"I would be happier, Jupiter, if you didn't come to breakfast in your swimming trunks," said Aunt Mathilda Jones.

Jupiter Jones pushed back the sleeves of his sweat shirt and reached for his orange juice. "I'm going swimming with Bob and Pete," he said. "They'll be here any minute."

Across the table, Uncle Titus Jones brushed a crumb from his big black mustache. "Don't eat too much," he warned Jupiter. "You're not supposed to swim on a full stomach."

"You don't want to get a cramp," said Aunt Mathilda. She then moved her coffee cup to one side and began to page through the *Los Angeles Times.*

Jupiter took a single slice of toast.

"Well, my gracious to Betsy!" said Aunt Mathilda. Then she sighed.

Jupiter looked up in interest. Aunt Mathilda was not much given to sighing.

"I was seventeen the year that movie came out," said Aunt Mathilda. "I saw it at the Odeon."

Uncle Titus looked blank.

"I don't think I slept for a week after," said Aunt Mathilda. She passed the paper across the table to Uncle Titus. Jupiter stood up and looked over his uncle's shoulder at the picture of a thin man with high cheekbones, pinched nostrils and piercing, dark eyes. In the photograph, the man stared intently into a glowing crystal ball.

"Ramon Castillo in *The Vampire's Lair*," said Jupiter. "He was a great master of make-up."

Aunt Mathilda shuddered. "You should have seen him in *Cry of the Werewolf*."

"I did," said Jupiter. "It was on television last month."

Uncle Titus finished reading the news story that accompanied the photograph of the late great character actor. "It says here that the auction of Castillo's estate will be held on the twenty-first," said Uncle Titus. "I think I'll go."

Aunt Mathilda pondered this, frowning slightly. She knew that Uncle Titus dearly loved auctions. She also knew that The Jones Salvage Yard, which she and Uncle Titus owned, was famous for its stock of hard-to-find items. People came to the yard seeking everything from steel beams and old bathtubs to antique sundials. Nevertheless, some of Uncle Titus's more unusual purchases had been difficult to sell. Aunt Mathilda was a firm believer in making a profit.

"They're selling the entire Castillo collection," said Uncle Titus. "All of his costumes and even the crystal ball he used in *The Vampire's Lair*."

"There are dealers who specialize in that sort of thing," Aunt Mathilda said. "Besides, the bidding will be high."

"I suppose so." Uncle Titus put the paper aside. "The collectors will be out in droves."

"I'm sure they will." Aunt Mathilda stood up and began to clear the table. Halfway to the sink she paused and listened. From the street outside came the clip-clop of hoofs. "The little Jamison girl," decided Aunt Mathilda.

Jupiter went to the window. It was the Jamison girl, and as usual she was astride her Appaloosa. The horse stepped along with its head high. It was a magnificent mare, brown with white markings on its hindquarters. "Beautiful horse," said Jupiter. "Typical of the Appaloosa breed."

He did not comment on the rider—the girl who sat straight in the saddle and looked neither to left nor right.

"Going for a gallop on the beach, I guess," said Aunt Mathilda. "That must be a lonely child. Marie told me her parents are in Europe."

"I know," said Jupe. Marie was the Jamison maid, and she and Aunt Mathilda were friends. On her afternoons off, Marie often came to have tea with Aunt Mathilda and to tell of the doings of the Jamison family.

Thanks to Marie, Jupe knew that when Mr. Jamison bought the old Littlefield mansion some months before, he spared no expense in having the place restored. He knew that the chandelier in the dining room had once graced a palace in Vienna, and that Mrs. Jamison had a diamond necklace which had once graced the throat of the Empress Eugénie. He knew that the girl on the Appaloosa was Allie, the Jamison daughter, and that the mare was her personal property. Jupe even knew that at the moment an aunt of Allie's from Los Angeles was presiding over the grand household, and in Marie's opinion, the aunt was very odd.

The girl and the horse disappeared around the corner, and Aunt Mathilda put the dishes she was holding on the drainboard. "You could try being nice to that girl," she told Jupe. "The Jamisons only live three blocks down the street. We're practically neighbors."

"She doesn't seem especially neighborly," said Jupe. "I think she only talks to horses."

"Perhaps she's shy," said Aunt Mathilda.

Jupe didn't reply, for Bob Andrews and Pete Crenshaw had come swooping down the street on their bikes. Like Jupe, Bob and Pete wore scuffed sneakers, swimming trunks and sweat shirts.

"See you later," said Jupe to his aunt, and he hurried out to meet the other boys.

The three were off then, with Jupiter pumping furiously at his bicycle. Jupe had once been a child actor, and had been called Baby Fatso. It was still easy to see why. In spite of his extra weight, however, he was ahead of Bob and Pete when they reached the corner of the street and turned down the short hill toward the Coast Highway.

Suddenly, "Watch out!" shouted Pete.

A horse screamed in terror. Jupe saw a huge shape rear in front of him. He threw his arms over his head, and as he fell he wrenched himself to one side. His bike clattered away.

There was another scream. It was thinner and higher— not an animal scream.

An instant later, hoofs struck the macadam very close to Jupe's head.

Jupe rolled away, then sat up. The Appaloosa was backing and prancing, ears flat against its head. The Jamison girl was lying on the road.

Bob and Pete dropped their bikes and Jupe scrambled up. All three hurried to the girl. Pete bent and touched her on the shoulder.

The girl was gasping, struggling to catch her breath. With a convulsive effort, she managed to get her lungs full of air. Then she shouted, "Take your hands off me!"

"Hey!" said Bob gently. "Take it easy, huh?"

She came to a sitting position and clutched at her knee, where blood streamed through a rip in her faded jeans. Her eyes were dry, but she was panting, almost sobbing.

"You really got the wind knocked out of you," said Pete.

She ignored him and glared at Jupiter. "Don't you know horses have the right of way?" she demanded.

"I'm sorry," said Jupe. "I didn't see you."

The girl stood up slowly. She looked at her mare and then back at Jupiter. Her eyes were pale—the same tawny color as her long hair—but at that instant they were cold with rage. "If you hurt my mare . . ." she began.

"I don't believe the horse is damaged in any way," said Jupiter stiffly.

The girl limped toward the Appaloosa. "Easy, girl!" she called. "Here, girl! Easy!"

The mare came to her and put its big head down on her shoulder.

"Did they scare you?" asked the girl. Her hands went up to stroke the horse's mane.

Aunt Mathilda appeared at the top of the road. "Jupiter? Pete? Bob? What's going on?"

The Jamison girl patted the horse again, reached up to grasp the saddle and tried to mount. The horse took a step backward.

"Hold it for her, Pete," said Jupe. "I'll give her a hand."

"I don't need a hand!" snapped the girl.

Aunt Mathilda came down the road. She stared at Allie Jamison—at the tangle of hair, the torn jeans, the bleeding knee. "What happened?"

"They scared my horse," said the girl.

"And she fell off," added Pete.

"It was an accident," said Jupe.

"I see. Jupiter, go and tell your Uncle Titus to bring one

of the trucks. I'll drive Miss Jamison home so she can have that knee attended to."

"I don't need anyone to drive me home," said Allie Jamison.

"The truck, Jupiter," said Aunt Mathilda. "And Pete, you hold the reins on that horse."

"Does it bite?" asked Pete.

"Certainly not," declared Aunt Mathilda, who really knew very little about the subject. "Horses don't bite. They kick."

"Oh, great!" groaned Pete.

The Night Visitor

2

When Bob, Pete and Jupiter led the Appaloosa up to the Jamison house, the truck from the salvage yard was standing in the brick driveway. Aunt Mathilda and the Jamison girl were nowhere to be seen.

Pete looked at the massive pillars that supported the roof over the veranda. "Too bad Aunt Mathilda didn't wear her hoop skirt today," he said.

Jupiter chuckled. "It does look like an old Southern mansion," he conceded.

"A big old Southern mansion," said Bob. "Where do you suppose we find the horse department?"

Pete pointed toward the rear of the property. "There's a field with a fence around it."

"Fine," said Jupe. They led the mare up the drive, past a flagstone patio which was shaded by a wisteria vine.

Behind the house, the brick driveway fanned out to become a courtyard. Next to the fenced field was a triple garage. One double door stood open, and inside there was a stall. Pieces of tackle hung from pegs on the walls.

The back door of the house opened and Marie, the

maid, looked out. "Boys, would you take the saddle off Indian Queen and let her into the field? Then come in. Miss Osborne wants to see you."

Marie disappeared into the house, closing the door behind her.

Pete looked at the mare. "Indian Queen?"

"I believe Allie Jamison calls her Queenie," said Jupe. "That's what Marie told Aunt Mathilda."

"Who's Miss Osborne?" asked Bob.

"She's the aunt who's staying here while Mr. and Mrs. Jamison are in Europe," Jupe told him. "According to Marie, she's rather peculiar."

"Peculiar how?"

"I don't know exactly, but Marie thinks there's something odd about her. If we're going to meet her, we can judge for ourselves."

Jupe removed the mare's saddle. Bob opened the gate to the field, and the horse trotted into the grass beyond the fence. Jupe found a stand in the garage for the saddle and a peg for the bridle. Then the boys opened the back door of the house and stepped directly into a huge, sunny kitchen.

They went through the kitchen to a wide central hall with a staircase. To the left was the dining room, and the boys looked out past the crystal drops of the famous chandelier to the wisteria-shaded patio. To the right of the hall was the living room which was all green-gold paleness. Beyond the living room, a door opened onto a paneled room lined with books.

Allie Jamison was in the living room stretched out on a sofa with a towel under her leg. Beside her sat a woman who might have been Aunt Mathilda's age, or perhaps a bit older. She wore a long gown of purple velvet, trimmed at the throat with a band of silver. Her hair was a delicate shade of lavender.

"Aunt Pat, Mom will kill me if I bleed on the sofa," said Allie. "Look, I'll go upstairs and . . ."

"Now dear, just lie still. You've had a shock." The woman did not look up at the boys, and Jupe saw that her hands shook as she cut the leg of the girl's jeans up from the ankle. "Oh, my. It's still bleeding," she said.

"A nasty scrape," said Aunt Mathilda, who had established herself in a chair near the fireplace. "Still, children do survive these things."

"I'll need some cobwebs," said the woman.

"Cobwebs?" echoed Aunt Mathilda.

"Cobwebs?" said Marie, who stood by holding a basin of water.

Bob and Pete shifted uneasily, and Pete looked questioningly at Jupe. Jupe smiled. "Cobwebs," he said to Marie. "Spiders make them."

Marie went pink with outrage. "There are no cobwebs in this house. I spray every week."

"Oh, how unfortunate," said the lady in purple. "Well, in that case, bring the gold jar from my medicine cabinet."

Marie went, and for the first time the woman in purple focused on the boys. "Thank you for helping my niece," she said. "Of course, this whole thing could have been prevented if she'd worn her purple scarf. Purple is for protection, you know."

"Of course," said Jupiter.

Marie returned with a small gilt jar.

"This should do it," said Allie's aunt. "It's not quite as good as cobwebs, but it *is* good. I made it myself." She took the lid from the jar and applied a clear ointment to Allie's knee.

"Would the American Medical Association approve?" asked Allie.

"Now, dear, it's sure to work," said Miss Osborne. "I gathered the herbs in the dark of the moon. Look. The bleeding's stopped."

"I hate to say so, Aunt Pat," said the girl, "but it stopped before you put that gunk on. What now? Do we order a wheelchair?"

"I think a bandage . . ." began Miss Osborne.

"I'll take care of it. It's no big deal." Allie got up and headed for the hall. She passed the boys as if they were invisible, then paused at the foot of the stairs. "Thanks," she said. "I mean, thanks for bringing Indian Queen home."

"No trouble," said Pete, who had stayed as far away from the horse as possible.

Allie went upstairs.

"I'm sure Allie is really grateful," said Miss Osborne. "She's a bit upset now, and you've been so kind and . . . and I'm afraid I didn't get your names."

Aunt Mathilda stood up. "I am Mrs. Titus Jones and this is my nephew, Jupiter Jones. And Pete Crenshaw and Bob Andrews."

Miss Osborne stared at Jupe, her violet eyes wide. "Jupiter Jones! Why, you're Baby Fatso!"

Jupiter did not care to be reminded of his stage name. He felt his face getting hot.

"The world's youngest has-been," said Pete with a smile.

"Ah, but to have been part of the wonderful world of cinema!" exclaimed Miss Osborne. Then her eyes went past Jupiter to the window. "It's Mr. Ariel!" she cried.

Aunt Mathilda and the boys turned to look. Out on the street, a man dressed in a black suit was getting out of a taxi. He had, thought Jupiter, the palest face ever seen on a human being. He looked as if he spent all his days in some deep cave.

Carrying a suitcase, the man headed up the drive to the walk leading to the front door.

"He *is* coming to stay after all!" Miss Osborne was obviously thrilled. "I was so hoping."

"We won't intrude," said Aunt Mathilda. "We must be going anyway." And before Miss Osborne could say one more word, she was shepherding the boys out the front door and across the veranda. They passed the black-clad man on the walk.

Aunt Mathilda paused before she climbed into the cab of the pickup truck. "If you boys are going swimming, you'd better go," she said. "Do you want a ride back to your bikes?"

"No thanks," said Jupe. "We'll walk."

Aunt Mathilda shook her head. "Never in all my life! Cobwebs on a wound! What an idea!" She climbed into the truck and slammed the door.

"It's an old folk remedy for bleeding," said Jupiter, who read a great deal and had a head crammed with odd bits of information.

"Dreadful!" announced Aunt Mathilda, and she backed the truck out of the drive.

"And peculiar," said Pete. "Marie is right. Allie Jamison's aunt is one very peculiar lady."

"She is, at least, very superstitious," said Jupiter.

He dismissed the subject of Allie Jamison from his mind then. Not until late that night, as he was falling asleep, did he think again of the Jamison house and the jar of ointment—herbs gathered in the dark of the moon. He smiled and pulled the bedclothes up to his chin. He was almost asleep when the pounding began at the door.

"Mrs. Jones! Mrs. Jones, let me in!"

Jupiter sprang out of bed, snatched his robe and charged into the hall. Aunt Mathilda was halfway down the stairs, with Uncle Titus behind her. Jupe followed and saw his aunt unlock the door.

Marie, the Jamison maid, almost fell into the house. "Oh, Mrs. Jones!" she wailed. She was in her bathrobe and slippers.

"Marie, what is it?" asked Aunt Mathilda.

"Can I stay here tonight?" pleaded Marie. She collapsed into a chair and began to weep.

"Marie, what *is* the matter?"

"The singing!"

"What?" said Aunt Mathilda.

"The singing." Marie twisted her hands. "There's something in that house and it's singing." She grasped Aunt Mathilda's arm. "It was horrible. Not like anything I ever heard. I can't go back there!"

The Insistent Client

3

As gently as she could, Aunt Mathilda released herself from Marie's grip. "I'm going to call the Jamison house," she announced.

Marie sniffled. "Call if you want," she said. "But I'm not going back!"

Aunt Mathilda dialed the Jamisons' number and reached Miss Patricia Osborne. The conversation was brief. "Miss Osborne says she didn't hear anything strange," Aunt Mathilda reported when she hung up the telephone.

"Miss Osborne *would* say that!" exclaimed Marie.

"What do you mean?" asked Aunt Mathilda.

"I mean . . . I mean she's peculiar and there's peculiar things going on in that house and I'm never going back. Not for anything!"

Marie would talk of it no more, and she didn't go back. She spent the night in the spare bedroom. In the morning Uncle Titus went to the Jamison house and collected her suitcases, which Allie Jamison had packed. Uncle Titus then drove Marie to her mother's home in Los Angeles.

"I wonder what Marie heard," said Jupiter Jones after she had departed.

Aunt Mathilda only shrugged.

Jupiter was still wondering several days later when he walked across the street from his house to the salvage yard in the middle of the morning. Hans and Konrad, the two Bavarian brothers who helped out at the yard, were cleaning a marble mantelpiece. Uncle Titus had bought it from the wreckers who were dismantling a burned-out house in the Hollywood Hills.

"Pete is in your workshop," said Hans.

"He want to use the printing press," added Konrad.

Jupe nodded. He did not need to be told that the press was in operation. He had assembled the press himself, out of old parts, and while the machine was efficient enough, it was noisy. He had recognized the familiar clanking and groaning the moment he came in the gate of The Jones Salvage Yard.

Jupe went quickly past piles of old lumber and stacks of steel beams to his outdoor workshop. It occupied a corner of the yard out of sight of the main area, which was Aunt Mathilda's special domain. The shop was sheltered from the street by the tall wooden fence that enclosed the entire yard, and it was partially sheltered from the weather by a six-foot-wide roof which ran all the way around the inside of the fence. Uncle Titus had built the roof to protect his most valuable junk.

In the workshop, Jupiter found Pete Crenshaw bent over the press, running off a stack of business cards. Jupe picked up one of the cards and examined it. It read:

THE THREE INVESTIGATORS
"We Investigate Anything"
? ? ?

First Investigator............................Jupiter Jones
Second Investigator......................Pete Crenshaw
Records and Research....................Bob Andrews

Pete stopped the press. "Satisfied, First Investigator?" he asked.

Jupiter nodded. "Very neat," he said. "And it's gratifying to know that the firm of The Three Investigators has been so successful. I wasn't sure, when we started, that we would ever need an additional supply of business cards."

Pete did not comment. He had been somewhat less than confident when he had joined with Jupiter Jones and Bob Andrews to found The Three Investigators. But Jupe's superior powers of deduction, Bob's talent for detailed research and his own athletic abilities had proved a powerful combination. The three young sleuths had been able to unravel mysteries which had seemed unsolvable to many of their elders.

The Investigators made their headquarters in a thirty-foot mobile home trailer which was hidden away behind piles of junk, not far from the workshop. Uncle Titus had given the trailer to the boys when he found it was too damaged to sell. They had since fixed it up to suit themselves.

Inside headquarters was a compact laboratory for analyzing physical evidence, and a photographic darkroom. There was an office for meetings, and a telephone which the boys paid for themselves out of money they earned helping in the salvage yard. And there were files in the trailer—files meticulously prepared by Bob—complete reports on the many cases the Investigators had undertaken.

"It hasn't been dull," said Pete at last.

"It has not," agreed Jupiter Jones. He looked at the business card in his hand, with its three question marks.

"The universal symbol of the unknown," he said. "The question mark is always intriguing. Mystery is always intriguing. I wonder, for example, about Marie."

"The Jamison maid?" questioned Pete.

"Yes. What did she hear in that house that frightened her? Was it something really strange, or did she let her imagination get the best of her? She said that Miss Osborne is peculiar, but she never explained why she thought so."

"Miss Osborne puts cobwebs on cuts," said Pete.

Jupiter suddenly held up a warning hand. There was a rustle beyond the heap of junk that separated the workshop area from the rest of the yard.

Pete strode quickly out of the workshop. An instant later, Jupe heard him exclaim mildly, "I thought I smelled a horse."

Allie Jamison stamped into the workshop area with Pete trailing her. "Very funny!" she said.

"How long have you been standing out there eavesdropping?" asked Jupe.

"Long enough," said the girl. Without waiting for an invitation, she sat down in an old chair near the press.

"Long enough for what?" said Jupe evenly.

The girl took a card from the stack on the printing press and looked at it. "My allowance will not stretch to cover a Pinkerton detective," she said. "What are your rates?"

"You want to retain The Three Investigators?" asked Jupe.

"Beginning right now."

"I'm afraid we'll have to know more about what's involved before we decide whether or not we're interested," said Jupiter Jones.

"You're interested, all right," Allie shot back. "I've been

listening to you two, and I know you're interested. You're dying to know what happened at our place the night Marie ran away. Besides, you don't have any choice."

"What's that supposed to mean?" asked Pete.

"You guys are getting careless," said Allie. "On the back fence of this place there's a painting of the San Francisco fire of 1905."

"It occurred in 1906," Jupiter informed her.

"Who cares? The important thing is that there's a little dog in that picture. I've been watching that fence. When you poke your finger through the knothole in the dog's eye, you can open a gate in the fence. You've got a secret entrance to this place. Does your aunt know?"

"Blackmail!" cried Pete.

"It is not blackmail," declared the girl. "I don't want money. I'll pay you. What I want is help, and I hear you're the best talent in town—not that that's saying heaps."

"Thanks a lot!" said Pete.

"You're welcome. Now, do you help me, or do I go and see your aunt?"

Jupiter sat down on an empty crate. "Exactly what do you have in mind?"

"I want to get that creep Hugo Ariel out of the house," said Allie quickly.

"Ariel? Isn't he the man who arrived the day you fell off the horse? A pale man dressed in black?"

"That's the one. The reason he's pale is that he never goes out in the daytime. His father must have been a mole."

"He arrived at your house the morning you fell. That night, Marie ran away." Jupiter pulled at his lower lip. "She did hear something strange," he suggested. "It wasn't her imagination."

"It sure wasn't." Allie Jamison suddenly seemed less

confident. She was folding the business card in her hand, creasing it nervously, then unfolding it again. "It had something to do with Ariel," she said slowly. "He's making that noise somehow, some way. I never heard that sound before he came."

"He's still there at your house?" asked Pete.

"He is, and my Aunt Pat seems to think he's keen. But then, Aunt Pat is totally off her rocker. Even before Ariel showed up, she used to draw a circle around her bed every night with a knife. That was to keep away evil influences. Now she's taken to lighting candles—lots of candles. They're very special candles. They're delivered from a shop in Hollywood and they're all colors. Purple is for protection and blue means something else and orange is good and red is very powerful. Every night Aunt Pat and Ariel go into the library and light candles and lock the door."

"And then?" prompted Jupiter.

"And then, sometimes, I hear that sound." Allie shuddered slightly. "I can hear it even if I'm upstairs, but I can hear it best if I'm in the living room. It comes out of the library."

"Marie said it was a singing noise," said Jupe.

Allie looked down at her hands. "I suppose you could call it singing, only . . . only I never heard any singing like it before. It's really eerie."

Jupiter frowned. "Marie said something was singing. She didn't say it was *someone,* she said it was *something.* She made it sound as if the noise wasn't made by a person."

Allie pulled herself erect in the chair and looked squarely at Jupiter. "Look, it doesn't matter. Ariel's doing it somehow and I can't stand it. It's got to stop!"

"Is it so bad?"

"It's bad. It's so bad we can't keep any help. The agency's sent two maids since Marie left. They won't stay. The place is knee-deep in dust and I'm starving to death, since I happen to be a rotten cook and Aunt Pat is worse. And I'm not allowed to make any noise because Ariel sleeps all day and wanders around the house all night. I don't like it and I want him out!"

"Getting rid of unwelcome house guests isn't exactly in our line," said Jupe. "I should think that if you had a talk with Miss Osborne . . . ?"

"I have talked with Aunt Pat until my throat hurts," said Allie. "She just smiles at me as if I had butterflies in my brain and changes the subject and talks about her old movie junk."

"Movie junk?" echoed Pete.

"She collects stuff from old movies," explained Allie. "She has everything from the fake eyelashes Della LaFonte wore in *Spring Fever* to the sword John Maybanks used in *Marko's Revenge.* Every time some movie star pops off or decides to move and get rid of his stuff, Aunt Pat is right there at the auction. That's where all her money goes."

"It sounds like a harmless hobby," said Jupe.

"So does lighting candles," Allie pointed out. "Only if Ariel comes with the candles, I draw the line. He's too much. He's got to go—him and his horrible noise!"

Pete leaned back against the printing press. "You know, Jupe, it could be kind of fun," he said. "We could short-sheet Ariel's bed and put frogs in his bathtub and gartersnakes in his shoes."

Allie snorted. "Ariel would love gartersnakes. What I want to do is get something on him!"

"Blackmail again?" said Jupe quietly.

"He asked for it, horning in in *my* house. Only I can't find out anything about him. He doesn't talk to me—he doesn't even seem to see me. And Aunt Pat won't tell me anything. There's something funny about him, and she doesn't want me to know what it is."

"But if she already knows—" began Pete.

"What she knows can't be real bad," interrupted Allie, "or she wouldn't have him around. She's kind of a dimwit, but she's not bad. What I want is some information I can clout him with. I need to know where he came from and what he's up to. That's where you come in.

"Now listen, tonight Aunt Pat's giving a party. She's been on the telephone inviting people and Ariel has been stirring up some brew for a punch. If there's going to be a party, there will be other people in the house and maybe they'll give us some lead to Ariel. So, since it *is* my house, you're invited to the party."

"Do we taste the punch?" asked Pete.

"No. You don't mingle. You observe. Then you track the guests to their lairs, or whatever we decide is best. I'll meet you at eight o'clock out by the garage. Cut across the back so no one sees you from the house." She stood up. "You'd better be there," she warned, "or I'll have a talk with Mrs. Jones about that secret gate."

Jupe and Pete listened to her footsteps going away across the salvage yard. "We have a new client whether we want one or not," said Jupe.

He pushed aside a piece of grating behind the printing press, revealing a large corrugated pipe which was padded with odd scraps of carpeting. This was Tunnel Two, another of the secret passageways in the salvage yard. It led under the piles of junk that concealed the mobile home trailer of The Three Investigators. At the far end of the pipe, a trap door opened directly into Headquarters.

"What are you going to do?" asked Pete.

"I don't think Bob is working at the library this morning. I'll call him and tell him we're all invited to a party."

"I'll go with you," said Pete. "I want to nail down those loose boards in the back fence. I hate to give up Red Gate Rover, but with Allie Jamison in the neighborhood, I don't think we have much choice."

The Singing Serpent

4

It was dusk when Jupiter Jones, Pete Crenshaw and Bob Andrews strolled past the Jamison house.

"Not a large party," said Jupiter.

There were three cars parked in front of the house—an orange sports car, a green station wagon and a dusty, tan sedan.

Beyond the house, The Three Investigators cut up through a vacant lot to get to the garage behind the Jamison place. Allie Jamison was waiting for them. "The group has gathered," she announced. "They're in the dining room and the patio doors are open. Don't make any noise and follow me."

They stole across the bricked courtyard and down the drive to the patio, with its shadowing wisteria. At the edge of the patio, Allie stopped.

Jupiter held a branch of wisteria aside and looked past Allie's shoulder into the dining room.

What he saw was unlike any party he had ever seen. There were five people in the room, and they stood in a silent circle around the table. Miss Osborne wore a long purple garment with wide sleeves and a high neck. Opposite her was the man called Hugo Ariel. He was dressed all in black, as he had been when the boys first saw him. His pale face gleamed in the light from two tall red candles which had been inserted into heavy silver candlesticks. His black hair was cropped short, but it had been brushed forward so that little tendrils reached toward his heavy eyebrows.

To Ariel's left was a thin woman in an orange gown. Like Miss Osborne, she had tinted her hair, but she had chosen an unfortunate color. The harsh red clashed with her orange robe.

Opposite the red-haired woman was a blonde lady fairly bursting out of a pale green gown. And next to her was the fifth member of the party. He looked out of place. The others stood straight, waiting expectantly for something. He slumped. The others had obviously dressed carefully for the party. He hadn't. His jacket looked weary and worn, and the inch of T-shirt that showed above his sports shirt would have been better for a trip to the laundry. His sparse, graying hair needed cutting.

Allie beckoned to the boys to follow her up the drive. When they were a little distance from the patio she stopped. "Cozy bunch, huh?"

"Are they going to just stand there?" asked Pete.

"Beats me," said Allie. "I wandered around among the guests until Ariel started giving me his special fishy stare. The guy with the messy clothes owns a delicatessen and his name's Noxworth. The skinny freak in the orange dress is Madelyn Enderby, Aunt Pat's hairdresser. She says she vibrates well in orange. I guess she does. At least she twitches a lot. The blonde owns a health food store."

Faintly, from the direction of the patio, came the sound of hands clapping.

"Something's up," whispered Allie. "Let's go."

The Three Investigators and Allie returned to the patio and peered in past the wisteria in time to see Miss Osborne hand Ariel a crystal goblet filled with an almost colorless liquid. Ariel took the goblet without looking at her and held it out toward the burning candles. His face was like a mask, as white as plaster and without expression. Only his eyes moved; they glinted darkly in the candlelight.

"We can begin," said Ariel.

The people gathered around the table shifted slightly, and Jupe thought he heard someone sigh.

"We are not the full fellowship tonight," said Ariel. "It may be that we can do nothing, or it may be that Dr. Shaitan will send us his spirits. The voice of the serpent may speak to us across the miles. We can try."

He touched the goblet to his lips, then passed the drink on to the woman in orange.

"The fellowship won't fail!" croaked the woman in orange. She sipped from the cup. "Why, when I had that trouble with my landlady, I—"

"Silence!" said Ariel. "You interrupt the rites."

She subsided and handed the cup to Miss Osborne, who sipped and passed it to the seedy Mr. Noxworth. He tasted it, gave it to the blonde in green, and she returned it to Hugo Ariel.

"We will be seated," said Ariel.

Each member of the party took a chair.

"Miss Osborne, state your intention," commanded Ariel.

Aunt Pat bowed her head. "I wish for the crystal ball. I wish that Margaret Compton will be called away so she can't get it."

"Shall we invoke the power of Belial?"

"I ask that this be done," said Aunt Pat.

Ariel looked around the table. "What do you say?" he asked the others.

"I've got problems of my own," said Noxworth.

"The problems of one are the problems of all the fellowship," Ariel reproved him.

"Let's ask Belial to send the Compton woman on a nice long trip," twittered the woman in orange. "A trip beginning . . . when was it, honey?"

"The week of the twenty-first," said Aunt Pat.

Ariel's dark eyes went from Aunt Pat to the blonde, and then to Noxworth. "Then we are agreed," he decided.

He leaned back in his chair and closed his eyes. The others sat, staring at the dancing flames of the candles. For some minutes, nothing happened. The figures in the dining room might have been painted on canvas, they were so still.

Then Allie and the boys heard it. In the night, through darkness which was now almost complete, they heard the sound. It was faint at first, a soft throbbing. It was a pulsing that seemed to stir the air. It was a singing sound, and yet it was in no way a song. There were no words. There were no syllables. There was only a rising and falling of notes that were no true notes. It was shrill, then gentle. It was high and piercing, then a low murmur. It wavered and stopped for an instant, then burst forth again in hideous gurgling waves.

The Three Investigators listened in mounting panic. The awful song was like nothing on earth. It threatened them with evil and terror and deep, dark power. It enticed them to join its own mindless agony. Bob swallowed noisily, and Pete drew a deep breath and held it.

Only Jupiter remained calm enough to concentrate on the scene before them. He noticed that no one had moved in the dining room. Hugo Ariel's face was turned toward the ceiling. He had not stirred.

At last Allie backed away from the patio. The boys went with her, retreating rapidly up the drive, the weird singing following them like some evil, living thing.

When they reached the back court, Allie leaned against the house. The boys felt the fear slowly drain from them.

"That was what Marie heard?" asked Jupe.

Allie didn't speak. She only nodded.

Pete ran his hand through his hair. "I'd leave, too," he said.

Allie breathed deeply. "I can't leave," she said finally. "It's my house, and it's my aunt. That Ariel has to go!"

"But it couldn't be Ariel," said Jupe quickly. "He couldn't make a noise like that without moving a muscle!"

"He couldn't make a noise like that at all, but he did it," said Allie flatly.

In the garage, the Appaloosa kicked against its stall and whinnied.

"Queenie!" cried Allie. "Someone's in there!"

Jupiter leaped to the garage door, threw it wide and was knocked flat on his back by someone who rushed out, struck wildly in the dark and fled, crashing through the lot next door.

"Jupe?" Pete knelt on the bricks.

"I'm all right." Jupe got up slowly. "Did you see who that was?"

"Chunky guy," said Bob. "Not too tall. Had a bushy mustache. Maybe a walrus mustache."

Allie regarded them with some respect. "You don't miss much. How could you tell in the dark?"

"There is a moon," Jupiter pointed out. "And investigators must have quick powers of observation," he added pompously. "For instance, have you noticed that the sing-ing has stopped?"

A light came on in the kitchen, and the boys slid into the shadows beside the garage.

The kitchen door opened. "Who's out there?" called Pat Osborne.

"It's only me, Aunt Pat," said Allie. "I was checking on Queenie."

"You do fuss about that horse," said Miss Osborne. "Come in, right away." The kitchen door closed.

From the front of the house came the sound of a car starting.

"The party's breaking up," whispered Bob.

"Come back in the morning," said Allie softly.

"We will," promised Jupe, and Allie's sneakered feet whispered off across the bricks to the house.

"Let's scram," said Pete. "And if I never hear that sound again, it will be okay with me!"

The Mysterious Fellowship

5

The next morning, The Three Investigators leaned on the fence and watched Allie Jamison's Appaloosa browse in its private meadow. "Some people don't have it that good," remarked Pete.

"Most people don't eat grass," said a voice behind them.

The boys turned to see Allie, clad in her usual faded jeans, but wearing a freshly ironed shirt. If she had been frightened the night before, she had recovered. The look she sent them was challenging. "Well?" she said. "Any bright ideas?"

Jupiter Jones glanced at the Jamison house. "Did anything happen after we left last night?"

"Nope," said Allie. "No crazy singing. No mysterious intruders with mustaches. Nothing." Allie climbed up to straddle the fence. "What about that man who was hiding in the garage? What do you think he was up to?"

Bob smiled at her and shook his head. "We don't know a thing about him, and without any facts, we can only guess. He might be an ordinary sneak thief looking for a way to get into the house, or he might be a tramp looking for a place to bed down for the night."

"Or he might have something to do with that weird sound," suggested Jupiter Jones. "Hugo Ariel spoke of the voice of the serpent coming across the miles."

"But serpents don't sing," said Allie. "They hiss."

"You never heard the noise before Ariel came to the house," reasoned Jupe, "so Ariel must be responsible for it in some way. Yet last night, when the singing began, he was sitting in your dining room in plain view and he wasn't making a move. In fact, he seemed to be in some sort of trance. He couldn't be the singer. The noise must be produced in some other fashion."

"How about a tape recording?" put in Pete. "They're doing terrific things with sound now. If Ariel's using taped sound, the man in the garage could be an accomplice. He could have planted the equipment near the dining room. He could have been waiting until the session was over, planning to get it back, only we scared him off."

"That's possible," said Jupe, "but we'd better not leap to any conclusions. Ariel may have no connection with the mustached intruder. He wouldn't really need an accomplice if he was using tape."

Allie hunched her shoulders. "So we're back where we started, and Ariel continues to get free room and board here. I don't care much for some of Aunt Pat's other friends, either."

"The other guests last night?" said Jupe. "That man Noxworth looked like an odd character."

"You might say that. How can he possibly run a delicatessen? He ought to be exterminated by the Board of Health!"

"He is slovenly," said Jupiter in his precise way. "Yet from what Ariel said last night, he and your aunt are members of the same fellowship, whatever it may be. And last night the guests were all united in wishing that someone

named Compton would be called away during the week of
the twenty-first so that your aunt could obtain a crystal
ball."

"Crazy!" exclaimed Allie. "Absolutely crazy!"

Jupiter permitted himself a somewhat superior smile. "I
think I know which crystal ball it is."

"You do?"

"On the twenty-first, there will be an auction of the estate of the late Ramon Castillo, the movie star. Among the
things to be sold is the crystal ball he used as a prop in the
film *The Vampire's Lair.* My aunt and uncle were discus-
sing it the other day. Your aunt collects items used in famous films. Wouldn't she want that crystal ball?"

"Her mouth must be watering at the idea!" said Allie.

"And she wants a person named Compton to be away
from the city at the time of the auction."

"Aunt Pat and Margaret Compton hate each other's
guts," said Allie.

"Is Margaret Compton also a collector?"

"She's a collector, all right, a very successful one. She's a
rich widow and has much more money than Aunt Pat. If
she wants that thing, she can bid it up so high that Aunt
Pat won't be able to touch it."

"And Hugo Ariel, by lighting candles and making
strange sounds, is going to prevent the Compton woman
from attending the auction."

"Nice of him," said Allie, "but why is he doing it? It
can't be for money. Aunt Pat has a little income from
stocks, but that's all. If she has to fuss about a high bid on
a crystal ball, she isn't going to have much to give Ariel, is
she?"

"So we don't know the motive," said Bob.

"But we do have an objective," countered Jupiter. "We
want to get Hugo Ariel out of Allie's house. We can't be

sure that Ariel has an accomplice, so let's assume that he doesn't. If we could search the house, we might find the equipment he uses to produce his night songs. We could then demonstrate this to your aunt, Allie. I think this should cause her to lose faith in him."

Allie grinned wickedly. "She'd toss him out on his ear. Great idea! And searching the house will be a cinch, because today Ariel got a phone call."

"Is that unusual?" asked Jupiter.

"It is. He never gets any calls. He never goes anywhere. But this morning the phone rang and a man asked for Ariel. I had to bang on his door to get him up."

"I'm sure you got to an extension and listened," said Pete slyly.

"No time," said Allie. "He was only on the phone for a couple of seconds. He said, 'Very good,' and hung up, and he told Aunt Pat that tonight there will be a meeting of the entire fellowship."

"Haven't you asked your aunt anything about this fellowship?" said Bob.

"Of course I asked her, and a fat lot of good it did. She says it's a nice club she belongs to. She says it's sweet of me to take such an interest in her social life. And she's all excited. She's going out tonight, and Ariel's going with her. So if we want to search the house for the gizmo Ariel uses to make that sound, we won't have any interruptions."

Jupiter mused, pulling at his lip. "He might carry the thing on his person," he said. "In that case, we'd find nothing."

"Aren't you even going to try?" demanded Allie. "It could be under the rugs or in the drapes or . . ."

"Yes, it could," admitted Jupe. "How are you at searching houses?"

"Well, I've never done it," admitted the girl, "but it isn't the kind of thing you have to take courses for."

"Fine. Tonight, you search. Don't forget the garage, in case there is an accomplice. Look for anything unfamiliar —a fine piece of machinery, a miniature tape recorder, anything like that."

"I'm so glad I hired you," said Allie. "I get to do all the work."

"Look everywhere," Jupe instructed her. "It could be under the table or the sideboard or . . ."

"In the wisteria, maybe?" suggested Allie.

"Yes, in the wisteria. Don't fall off the trellis."

"Don't worry. And while I'm climbing around on that trellis, what are you going to be doing?"

"We will be following your aunt and Ariel to the meeting of the fellowship."

The House
at Torrente Canyon
6

"It was nice of you to bring your own car, Worthington,"
said Pete warmly.

Worthington smiled. He was piloting his trim Ford
sedan down the Coast Highway, several hundred yards behind the purple Corvette that belonged to Pat Osborne. "A
gold-plated Rolls-Royce is not the ideal automobile in
which to tail anyone," said Worthington.

Some time before, Jupiter had entered a contest spon-
sored by the Rent-'n-Ride Auto Rental Company and had
won the use for thirty days of an antique Rolls-Royce with
gold-plated trim. With the car had come Worthington, the
perfect English chauffeur. He had driven The Three Investigators during several of their cases. After the thirty days
had elapsed, a grateful client had arranged for the boys to
have unlimited use of the Rolls-Royce. By now, Worthington had become so interested in the work of Jupiter Jones,
Pete Crenshaw and Bob Andrews that he considered himself a part of the firm—an unofficial Fourth Investigator.
When Jupiter had called the auto rental agency that morning, the chauffeur had gladly offered to use his own car to

follow Miss Osborne and Hugo Ariel to the meeting of their mysterious fellowship.

Now, "She's turning onto Sunset Boulevard," said Worthington.

"Don't get caught on that traffic signal," warned Jupiter Jones, who sat next to Worthington.

"I shan't." Worthington flicked his turn signal and slid through the intersection just as the light clicked to orange. "I hope she reaches her destination before it gets too dark," he said, and he guided the Ford up the steep hill away from the ocean. Sunset Boulevard wound ahead, past trim homes and gardens bright with geraniums. The boys lost sight of the Corvette from time to time when the road curved, but it always came into view again. At last, the little car slowed.

"Torrente Canyon," murmured Worthington. "We can't lose her now. That's a dead-end road."

The Corvette turned into the canyon road, and an orange sports car spurted down Sunset and followed it. "Aunt Pat's hairdresser," said Jupiter.

"Just follow her red hair, Worthington," said Pete. "It probably glows in the dark."

Worthington chuckled and turned into Torrente Canyon Road. He followed the orange car until it pulled over and stopped on the grassy bank beside a high brick wall. There were other cars parked beside the road. The boys crouched low in the Ford as Worthington drove past the purple Corvette. Miss Osborne and Hugo Ariel were getting out.

Worthington looked into his rear-view mirror. "The woman in orange is waving to Miss Osborne."

Bob and Pete twisted around to look out the back window. "I see the tan car that was in front of Allie's house last night," said Bob.

"The delicatessen man," guessed Pete. "There sure are a lot of people here tonight."

Worthington let the Ford drift to the right and brought it to a stop on the unpaved shoulder of the road. "I counted eleven cars," he said.

The boys looked back and saw the red-haired woman join Ariel and Pat Osborne outside a huge iron gate with spikes on the top. Ariel spoke briefly to the two women, then stepped to the wall near the gate. He reached up and took something from a niche in the wall.

"I think that's a telephone," said Bob.

It was a telephone. Ariel held the receiver to his ear, listened, then said a few words and replaced it in the niche. Seconds later, the watchers in the car heard a strident buzz. Hugo Ariel leaned on the gate and it swung open. The two women followed him through and the gate closed behind them.

Worthington and the boys waited, not speaking. No more cars appeared on Torrente Canyon Road. No one else approached the big gate. After fifteen minutes, Jupiter opened the door of the Ford. "The gathering of the fellowship must be complete," he announced. "It now remains for us to discover what kind of fellowship it is."

The others got out of the car and followed Jupe to the gate in the brick wall. "Your Uncle Titus would love to have this," said Bob admiringly, touching one of the scrolls which decorated the gate.

"I doubt that it's for sale," said Jupiter. He took hold of the polished brass handle and tried to force it down, then up. It would not budge. "Locked," he said. "I expected as much."

Pete was investigating the niche near the gate. "Shall we try the phone?" he said. "No dial. It must connect directly with the house."

"I say, Master Pete," warned Worthington.

Pete grinned and took the phone off its hook. He heard a clicking noise, and then, "The night is dark," said a voice on the telephone.

"Ah . . . well, yes, it soon will be," said Pete. "Sir, I represent the United Cookie Company, and this week we're offering a special on chocolate—"

The phone clicked and went dead.

"They aren't interested in cookies?" asked Jupe.

"They sure aren't." Pete replaced the receiver. "Darnedest way to answer a phone I ever heard. You know what he said? He said, 'The night is dark.' "

"Part of a password, no doubt," said Jupiter. "If we were members of this fellowship, we would know what to answer."

Bob looked in through the gate. "It *is* getting dark," he said, "and look at that house. You can just make it out up at the end of the drive. There isn't a single light in the place."

It was true. No windows glowed in the house. It appeared only as a hulking mass against the evening sky.

"There are eleven cars parked on the road," said Jupe. "Two of the cars brought three people—the three we saw go in through the gate. That means there are at least nine more people visiting that house. Twelve in all."

"What are they doing?" asked Worthington. "There should be *some* light."

"There may be heavy drapes," said Jupiter.

"And they could be using candles," Bob pointed out. "Candles seem to be important to these people, and they wouldn't show through drapes."

The Three Investigators stood in the darkening road and thought of the group that had gathered at the Jamison house the night before, of the candles glowing in the dining room and the goblet that had been passed from one person to another. And they thought of the sound they had heard—the terrible, tuneless singing.

"I wonder if we'll hear it tonight," said Pete, almost to himself.

"Hear what?" asked Worthington.

"We aren't sure, Worthington," said Jupiter. "We think it's what Ariel calls the voice of the serpent. However, we'll never learn anything standing here."

"There might be another gate," said Bob.

"There might," agreed Jupe, "and it might even be unlocked. Most people are very particular about the locks on their front doors, but very few bother about their back doors. It's a thing that causes the police no end of work."

"All right," said Pete. "Let's go and see."

"Worthington, why don't you stay in the car and keep the motor running?" said Jupe. "We don't know anything about this fellowship. It's possible that we may have to leave, and leave quickly."

The chauffeur hesitated. "Very well," he said. "I'll turn the car around and keep the motor running." He walked away up the road, and the boys heard the door of the Ford open and close and the motor start. Headlights blinked on, and Worthington made his U-turn and coasted down past the gate. He went on for about fifty feet, then pulled to the side of the road. The headlights went out, and the road was suddenly very, very dark.

"I wish we'd brought a flashlight," said Pete.

"We're better off without one," Jupe told him. "We don't want to attract attention. Let's go."

The Three Investigators began a careful circuit of the brick wall. They walked slowly, stopping from time to time to listen. They heard no sound from beyond the wall. Once Bob jumped and almost cried out when some small creature scuttled across his feet and dashed away.

"A fox," said Pete quickly.

"Did you see it?" asked Bob.

"No, but let's just say it was a fox."

"Quiet!" warned Jupe.

But then they were back on the paved road. They passed Worthington and his softly purring car. They arrived at the big gate again. Their tour was finished and they had found nothing. There was no second gate. They knew only that the property was large—almost a block square—and that there were no near neighbors, and that the house at the head of the drive was still dark.

"We must get over that wall," decided Jupiter. "Pete, you're the athlete. I can lean on the wall and you can climb on my back."

"You're out of your mind!" declared Pete.

"I see no other way," said Jupe. "If you won't do it, I must, but it seems to me that you're the logical one. Once you get on top of the wall, you can help me up and we can help Bob. It's the only way we can get in to see what's happening in that house."

Pete sighed, as he had many times since joining Jupiter Jones and Bob Andrews. "I'm not sure I want to see," he muttered. But when Jupe bent, put his arms over his head and braced himself against the wall, Pete came through. He put one knee on Jupe's back, touched the wall with his hands, placed a sneakered foot on Jupe's shoulder and stood. "Here goes," he said, planting both hands on the top of the wall. He pulled himself up.

He sat on the wall a moment to survey the dark grounds around the darker house. Then it happened.

The alarm bell rang first—an ear-shattering, persistent clanging.

"Get down!" cried Jupe from the roadway.

Floodlights blazed suddenly. There were eight of them, two at each corner of the wall. Pete clutched at the bricks, caught and blinded by the blue-white glare.

"Jump!" shouted Jupiter.

Pete tried. He swung himself around and let his legs drop outside the wall. But then, under his hand, a brick slipped, gave way and fell. And Pete fell, too. Backward, inside the wall!

Caught!

7

Pete landed on his back on soft turf. He rolled a bit and brought himself to his knees. The alarm bell stopped clanging. Pete blinked and turned his head away from the glare of the floodlights.

A thickset man stood between Pete and the wall.

"You little sneak," said the man. He did not move, but his voice chilled Pete. "Just what do you think you're doing here?"

Pete opened his mouth to say something and found that his throat was suddenly very dry. He began to get up, and the man took a single menacing step toward him. Pete froze, half-crouching.

"Pete?" called Jupiter Jones from the other side of the wall. "Pete, did you find him?"

The man shifted and looked around. "Who's that?"

There were quick footsteps beyond the wall, and Jupe appeared at the gate. "Hey, mister," he said to the man who stood over Pete, "did you see him?"

Pete felt himself begin to relax. Jupiter Jones was putting on an act, and whatever act it was, Pete knew it would be a good one.

"See who?" asked the man.

"The cat," replied Jupiter brightly. "I'm going to get it if I don't find him. He's a seal point Siamese, and my mother doesn't know he's out. I saw him go over your wall."

"Tough!" said the man.

"He's probably up a tree someplace," said Jupe.

"Too bad." The man turned away from Jupe, pushed back a mane of gray hair with one hand, then scowled at Pete. "You, kid," he said. "Out!"

Pete stood up.

"Hey, please!" called Jupe. "Let me in and I'll help my friend look for the cat."

"Help him look my foot!" The man took Pete by the elbow and pushed him toward the gate.

"My mother will murder me!" protested Jupe.

"We've all got problems," snarled the man. "Beat it or I'll call the cops."

Jupiter retreated a step and watched. As the man neared the gate, his hand went out to touch something in the ivy that grew up the inside of the wall. The gate clicked.

"You come over that wall again and you're going to have more to worry about than a lost cat," said the man. He opened the gate and thrust Pete out onto the road, then slammed the gate shut.

"If you should see the cat . . ." began Jupe.

"Scram!" shouted the man.

Jupe and Pete turned and walked a few paces down the road to the place where Bob waited. The floodlights at the corners of the property blinked out, leaving them in darkness.

"Whew!" said Pete.

"Good thinking, Jupe," murmured Bob.

The boys heard the man go a few paces up the drive and then stop.

"He's waiting to make sure we leave," whispered Jupiter. "We'd better walk away, and Worthington can follow with the car. That man is already suspicious. If he sees us get into a car, he'll know we weren't simply looking for a stray cat."

"Let's go," said Pete quickly.

The boys straggled toward Sunset Boulevard, talking loudly of the elusiveness of cats, the value of Siamese in particular, and the dreadful fate that awaited boys who allowed their parents' pets to escape. As they came abreast of the Ford, Jupe whispered to Worthington to follow them in a few minutes.

The Investigators halted at Sunset and Torrente, well out of sight and hearing of the big house.

"Interesting household," said Jupiter. "There is a gathering there with at least twelve people present, but we saw no lights. There is an alarm system which I imagine is activated by an electronic device on top of that wall. And one needs a password to enter the gate."

The Ford came gliding down the road and stopped. The boys opened the doors and got in.

"A thoroughly obnoxious person!" exclaimed Worthington, waving his hand in the direction of the house.

"Could you hear him?" asked Pete.

"He was loud enough," said Worthington. "I was tempted to take steps. Did he hurt you, Master Pete?"

Pete slumped back in his seat. "No, but I don't think it would have bothered him if he had."

Worthington started to edge out into the traffic on Sunset Boulevard. There was a truck approaching from the left, and as Worthington waited for it to pass, a car spurted down Torrente Canyon Road and shuddered to a stop next to the Ford. The driver of the car gunned the motor impatiently.

"That's the orange sports car," said Bob. "The twitchy hairdresser is on her way."

"Then the group must be leaving," surmised Jupe. "We'd better get to a telephone right away. Allie is supposed to be searching her house for evidence against Hugo Ariel. We don't want Ariel and her aunt to find her at it."

Worthington turned onto Sunset. "There's a telephone booth at a gas station less than half a mile from here," he announced.

At the gas station, Jupe called the Jamison house. Allie answered before the phone could ring twice.

"The meeting of the fellowship is breaking up," said Jupe. "We found out almost nothing. Have you finished your search?"

"Yes, and I didn't find a thing."

"You looked everywhere?"

"I went over this place with a fine-tooth comb. I also used a magnet. There's nothing except the dust that's piled up since Marie took off."

"Then if Ariel uses some device to make that noise, he carries it with him," said Jupe. "Or perhaps he does have an accomplice."

"Which brings up an interesting point," said Allie brightly. "We have a new houseman."

"Oh?" said Jupe.

"Yes. Not a maid this time. A houseman. Tonight this man called and said he'd been in Rocky Beach and he heard we lost our maid and might need help, which we certainly do. He wanted to make an appointment to come and see the lady of the house."

"So?"

"So I figured, with my mom in Europe, I'm the lady of the house. Aunt Pat hardly takes a big interest, after all."

"Allie, you didn't make an appointment with a total stranger who called up without even—"

"I did better than that," said Allie proudly. "I asked him to come here and I hired him."

Jupe waited, feeling that there was more to come.

"Aren't you going to ask me why I hired him?" said Allie.

"Why did you hire him?"

"Because he has a walrus mustache," said Allie. "You said the man who was hiding in the garage last night had a walrus mustache. Now I don't know if this is the same man. I didn't get a good look at that guy last night. But if he *is* the same man, he must have some special interest in what goes on here. He could be an accomplice. So let's get him where we can keep an eye on him, huh? He reports to work at eight tomorrow morning, and I hope he gets eggshells into Ariel's morning coffee."

"What will your aunt say?" demanded Jupiter.

"I'll think of something clever to tell her. See you tomorrow out by the old corral."

She hung up and Jupe returned to the car.

"Allie okay?" asked Pete.

"I don't know," said Jupe. "Either she's the smartest girl I ever met, or she's an idiot, or maybe she's both."

"How can you be a smart idiot?" asked Pete.

"Somehow, I believe Allie Jamison could manage it," said Jupiter Jones.

The Serpent Strikes

8

When The Three Investigators arrived at the Jamison house the next morning, Allie was sitting on the front steps, grinning like a Cheshire cat.

"A dream of a man!" she announced. "Listen!"

Jupiter, Bob and Pete listened. From inside the house came the drone of a vacuum cleaner.

"I didn't even mention it to him," said Allie. "He stowed his suitcase in Marie's room, took one look around the house, went for the broom closet and got busy. So much for Aunt Pat's cobwebs."

"Then he'll be living here?" asked Bob.

"Isn't that nice?" said Allie. "We can really watch him."

"Let's hope it will be nice," replied Jupe. "What did your aunt say when you told her you'd hired a man for the house?"

"Whose house is it, anyway?" demanded Allie. "I told her I'd asked around and this man seemed okay, and she said that was nice of me, dear, and went to bed. She's fuzzy about details."

"Where has he worked before?" asked Jupiter.

"He didn't say and I never pry," said Allie, virtuously.

"The heck you don't!" exclaimed Pete.

"Want to see him?" asked Allie. "Think you can tell if he's the same man who was in the garage?"

"I doubt if I could," said Jupe. "I hardly saw him. Bob had the best look at him."

Bob nodded.

"If he is the man," said Jupe, "don't accuse him, Bob. Pretend not to recognize him."

Allie yanked open the screen door and the boys followed her into the house. The new houseman was laboring over the green-gold carpet in the living room. He looked up, saw the boys standing in the hall with Allie and switched off the vacuum.

"Was there something you wanted, Miss Jamison?" he asked.

"Not a thing, Bentley," said Allie. "We're going to get some soda."

"Very well, Miss Jamison." The man clicked the vacuum on again and continued with his work.

In the kitchen, Allie took four bottles of pop from the refrigerator. "Is it him?" she asked.

"I couldn't be sure," admitted Bob. "He's about the same size and the mustache looks right. But it was dark when that man knocked Jupe down and it all happened so quickly."

"He doesn't look like the kind who knocks people down," said Pete. "He's sort of . . . well, sort of neutral."

"Beige," said Allie. "He's a beige person. Not too tall and not too short and not too thin and not too fat. Sandy hair and eyes that aren't any particular color. He'd be invisible if he didn't have that mustache." She took a bottle opener from a drawer and began to remove the caps from the pop bottles. "And what have you three to report?"

Jupiter quickly outlined the events of the evening before. When he finished, Allie said, "I think I'm way ahead of you. All you managed to do last night was fall off a wall, while I found a genuine, one-hundred-percent mystery man."

"You came to us to get rid of a mystery man," Pete reminded her. "By the way, aren't you afraid that vacuuming is going to wake your house guest?"

"Ariel went out," said Allie, and swallowed some soda pop.

"I thought he never went out in the daytime."

"This morning he went out. He took Aunt Pat's car and departed for points unknown."

Aunt Pat appeared in the kitchen doorway.

"Allie, who is that man in the living room?" asked Miss Osborne. She was dressed in a lavender housecoat with a purple sash, and her lavender hair was perfectly arranged.

"It's the new houseman, Aunt Pat," said Allie. "We hired him last night, remember?"

"Oh, yes. How nice. What did you say his name was, dear?"

"I didn't," said Allie, "but it's Bentley."

"Bentley. Bentley. Like the car. I'll remember that." She smiled in an absent-minded way at the boys, who murmured good-morning to her.

"Can he cook?" Miss Osborne asked Allie.

"He said he could cook."

"Then I'll go and talk to him about dinner." Miss Osborne wandered out of the kitchen.

Allie leaned against the sink. "I don't care if he runs off with the silverware, just so we get one decent meal out of him. There's more to this pots and pans stuff than meets the eye." She turned her head and glanced out into the back court. "Speaking of things meeting the eye," she re-marked, "if you'll look to the east, you'll see that creep Ariel fighting his way out of Aunt Pat's car."

The boys had to smile. It was a struggle for Ariel to get his long legs out of the purple Corvette. He wriggled side-ways, slid out and pulled his black shirt straight about his thin waist.

"I'd love to know what he's been up to," said Allie.

Ariel opened the back door and came in. He let his flat, dark eyes rest on Allie for a moment, then started past her without speaking.

Allie promptly stood in his way. "Mr. Ariel, I don't think you've met my friends," she said.

Ariel looked intensely annoyed, but he stopped and per-mitted Allie to introduce the boys. When Bob cheerfully held out his hand, Ariel allowed his own limp hand to be shaken. He said absolutely nothing. When the introduc-tions were completed he stepped around Allie as if she were a post and went on into the hall, pulling the kitchen door shut after him.

"How'd you like that?" demanded Allie. "I get it from him all the time. He acts like I'm some kind of a . . . a thing! I'd want him out of here even if he didn't make that horrible singing."

"Mr. Ariel!" Aunt Pat's voice, high and excited, carried to the group in the kitchen. "Has it been accomplished?"

Allie went to the door, leaned on it slightly and applied her ear to the resulting crack.

"There is no need for anxiety," said Ariel from the front hall. "The wishes of the fellowship—your wishes—will be carried out. The serpent has been delivered. All is in the hands of Belial. You have only to wait."

"But the twenty-first isn't far off," protested Aunt Pat.

"Are you sure there's time? Oh, perhaps it is a silly whim, but I do want it, and if Margaret Compton gets there first . . ."

"Your faith wavers?" demanded Ariel. There was an edge to his voice.

"Of course not!" said Aunt Pat quickly. "I have the most profound trust."

"Then you will excuse me," said Ariel. "I must rest now. These affairs are demanding."

"I understand," said Miss Osborne.

Ariel went up the stairs.

"Sounds like he's sacking out for another day," said Allie. "What a slug!"

"The serpent has been delivered," said Jupe. "Now what did he mean by that?"

"Is somebody mailing out snakes?" asked Pete.

Allie shook her head. "Aunt Pat can't abide snakes. That's just the way they talk. They say something and it means something else. The other night they talked about the voice of the serpent coming across the miles, remember?"

"And we heard it, didn't we?" Jupiter reminded her. "We heard the singing."

"Whatever that was, it was no snake," insisted Allie. "Snakes do not sing."

"But something is going on," said Jupe. "It has to do with Hugo Ariel and the house on Torrente Canyon and that strange singing. And it may have some connection with your new houseman. There's nothing we can do at the moment except watch and wait. Let us know if something odd happens. I have to get back to the salvage yard."

"And I'm due at my job in the library," said Bob.

"And I've got to mow the lawn," said Pete.

"What a bunch of private eyes!" complained Allie.

"You've all got other jobs on the side. Okay. Go do whatever it is you do when you're not falling off walls and I'll call you if anything happens here."

The boys finished their pop and went their separate ways. When Jupiter reported at The Jones Salvage Yard, Aunt Mathilda was directing Hans and Konrad, who were unloading the larger of the two trucks.

"Jupiter, I need you," said Aunt Mathilda.

"Yes, Aunt Mathilda."

"Your Uncle Titus has lost his mind. Look what he bought!"

Jupiter looked. The truck was loaded with old cast-iron stoves.

"Wood-burning stoves!" said Aunt Mathilda. "In this day and age! They were in an old warehouse in East Los Angeles, and it was going to be torn down. Your uncle said they were so inexpensive he couldn't pass them up. Jupiter, however will we sell them?"

"We'll find a way," said Jupe.

"Well, help Hans and Konrad get them off the truck and put them someplace where I can't see them. The very idea!"

Aunt Mathilda stormed away, and Jupiter set to work helping Hans and Konrad unload the stoves and store them in a spot toward the back of the yard. It was slow work, since the stoves were heavy and had doors which kept dropping off. After lunch there were more chores. Jupe worked until three and then crossed the street to the Jones house to take a shower. He found his Uncle Titus glaring at a newscast on television.

"Terrible!" exclaimed Uncle Titus.

"What's terrible?" asked Jupiter.

"The things people do on the freeways. Look at that!"

On the television screen, Jupe saw a scene which was all

too familiar. A sedan had crashed into a bridge abutment on the Hollywood Freeway. The highway patrol was directing traffic past the wreck.

The voice of the announcer came on over the picture. "The driver of the car, Mrs. Margaret Compton, was taken to Angel of Mercy Hospital where her condition was reported as fair."

"Mrs. Margaret Compton!" cried Jupe.

"You know her?" asked Uncle Titus.

"I've heard the name, Uncle Titus," said Jupe. "Excuse me. I have to call a client!"

A Secret Meeting

9

At seven that night, Jupiter left the house and went to The Jones Salvage Yard. He had told his aunt that he had unfinished work in his workshop, and that he might be late. However, when he reached his workshop, Bob and Pete were waiting for him with their bikes.

"We're to meet Allie at Swanson's Cove," said Jupe quickly.

"We exit through Green Gate One?" asked Bob.

Jupe nodded. "We'd better. It's far enough from the house so Aunt Mathilda won't see us."

Pete went to a place in the fence right by the workshop and inserted two fingers into a crack. He pulled, and two boards swung up. Pete put his head out, looked up and down the street, and reported that the coast was clear. Jupe grabbed his bike, which had been leaning against the printing press, and the three boys slipped out through the opening in the fence.

When the boards had swung closed behind them, Bob stopped to stare thoughtfully at the fence. Like the back fence of the yard, the front fence had been decorated by artists of Rocky Beach. Here along the front was a stormy ocean scene, with a sailing ship struggling through huge waves. In the foreground, almost under Bob's eyes, a fish lifted its head from the sea to stare at the ship.

"Allie caught on to Red Gate Rover," said Bob sadly. "I hope she hasn't been snooping around the front of this place. I'd hate to have her know that that fish marks the spot where Green Gate One opens."

"If she's discovered that," said Jupiter Jones, "we'll have to abandon Green Gate One and construct another entrance. Let's not worry about it now. This is an emergency."

"Right," said Pete. "Let's go."

The boys got onto their bikes and pedaled down the street, away from the Jones house and the salvage yard, and then down to the Coast Highway. A five minute ride brought them to Swanson's Cove. Allie Jamison was already there, leaning against a boulder that jutted out of the sand. Allie's horse stood nearby, its reins dangling.

"Margaret Compton got hurt on the freeway today," said Allie.

"I told Bob and Pete about it," said Jupe. He sat down facing Allie. "How is your aunt? What's happened since I talked to you?"

"She's all upset," said Allie. "She's crying. She hasn't stopped crying since we caught the report on the news."

Bob leaned against the rock. "Things are moving, aren't they?" he said.

"And rather quickly," said Jupe. "Only this morning Hugo Ariel told Miss Osborne that a serpent had been delivered, and that Miss Osborne's wishes would be carried out. Tonight Mrs. Compton is in the hospital with more serious things to worry about than the auction of the Castillo estate. She won't be around to outbid Miss Osborne for Ramon Castillo's crystal ball."

"This isn't the way Aunt Pat wanted it," declared Allie. "When she saw the newscast she yelled, 'She might have been killed, and it would be my fault!' Ariel helped her up to her room. They closed the door, but I was out in the hall and I listened."

"Naturally," said Pete.

Allie ignored him. "She said something about how she didn't know it would turn out like this," Allie went on. "He said it was her desire, and now it was time for her to do something. I couldn't get it all, but whatever he wants, she doesn't want to do it. He said he'd wait, but not forever. After a while he came out and went downstairs.

"I went in after he left, but she wouldn't talk to me. She told me to run along, so I did, only I didn't run far."

"You stayed in the hall," said Pete.

"You bet I did, and I heard her making a telephone call. She asked to speak to Mr. Van Storen."

"How long did it take you to get to another telephone?" asked Jupiter Jones.

"Too long," confessed Allie. "By the time I picked up the receiver downstairs, she was telling someone she'd send in her houseman with a letter of authorization, and a man said, 'Certainly, Miss Osborne,' and everybody hung up."

"So then?" asked Bob.

"So then I heard Aunt Pat moving around upstairs. She called Bentley and he went up, and when he came down he was tucking a package all wrapped in brown paper into his pocket. He went out in Aunt Pat's car. Said she'd given him an errand to do."

"Did that interest Mr. Ariel?" questioned Jupe.

"It interested him plenty," said Allie. "He went up those

stairs like a shot out of a cannon. Aunt Pat was ready for
him. I could hear him yelling at her and she yelled back.
She said she'd sent Bentley to Beverly Hills to pick up
some special face cream for her, and that's all."

"Do you believe her?"

"No, and Ariel didn't either. Only Bentley came back
later with the face cream, so what could Ariel say? But it
was a lie. Aunt Pat doesn't buy face cream. She makes her
own out of rose petals and glycerine and stuff."

"Did you question your aunt?" asked Jupe. "Or did you
speak to Bentley?"

"I didn't need to question either of them," said Allie. "I
know where Bentley really went. Mr. Van Storen is one
half of the firm of Van Storen and Chatsworth in Beverly
Hills. He's a jeweler and a very good one. I also happen to
know the combination of the safe in my mother's room, so
I opened the safe. My mother's necklace was gone."

The boys sat silently on the sand for a moment, letting
this news sink in.

Jupiter spoke up at last. "Do you mean that your aunt
gave a necklace which once belonged to the Empress Eugénie to a man whom she scarcely knows and sent him to
the jewelers with it?"

"I never said she was real bright," said Allie. "She's a
grownup, so she's supposed to be responsible. So I guess
that's why my mother gave her the combination of the safe—
so she could get the necklace out in case the house burned
down or something."

"Does she know that you know the necklace is gone?"
asked Bob.

"She sure does. I nailed her the second I got her alone.
She claims my mother asked her to have the necklace
cleaned while she was away."

"Not a likely story?" asked Jupiter.

Allie made a wry face. "There's no emergency about having a necklace cleaned," she pointed out. "And she didn't need to send Bentley. Van Storen and Chatsworth would have come for it."

"So she went to some trouble to get the necklace to the jewelers without Ariel's knowledge," said Jupiter. "I think we can come to several conclusions."

"Such as?"

"First, from what your aunt said about the Compton woman's accident, it was caused—or she believes it was caused—because she wished the Compton woman out of the way. She invoked the power of the fellowship. She feels guilty.

"Second, Ariel is putting some pressure on her. He has stopped playing the role of an honored guest and is trying to bully her. Did he see the houseman with the package?"

"No," said Allie. "He only saw Bentley get into the car and drive away."

"Does he know the necklace was in the safe?"

"I don't know. I don't think so. He didn't try to go near the safe. He only wanted to know why Aunt Pat sent Bentley out."

"Which brings us back to the mysterious Bentley," said Jupiter. "Is he the man who was hiding near your house the night your aunt entertained her friends from the fellowship? Or is he a stranger who happened to learn that you needed household help? If he is the man who knocked me down that night, what is he doing in the house? At least we know he can't be an accomplice of Ariel's, or Ariel would not need to be suspicious of him." Jupe sat brooding, pulling on his lip as he did when he was thinking with special intensity.

"There are several things we must find out immediately," he decided. "We must find out, first of all, whether the necklace was actually delivered to the jewelers."

"Oh, blast!" cried Allie. "Oh, why didn't I think of that this afternoon? I could have called Van Storen and Chatsworth right away!"

"In the morning," advised Jupiter. "You can call from the salvage yard, if you want, so no one will overhear. And in the morning we must find out whether Margaret Compton's accident was truly connected with the fellowship. Did Ariel deliver a live snake to her, for instance?"

"But Aunt Pat wouldn't send anybody a snake!" protested Allie. "She doesn't like Margaret Compton, but she wouldn't wish a thing like that on her. She wouldn't want her worst enemy to open a box and see a snake!"

"Then what was delivered?" said Jupe.

"I don't know."

Bob spoke up. "Ariel said that your aunt didn't need to worry because it was all in the hands of Belial. I looked that up in the library. Belial is the name of a demon. And Ariel mentioned a Dr. Shaitan the other night. I checked that, too, in the library. Shaitan is another name for Satan."

Pete shivered. "Demons and snakes! Some combination!"

Allie sat, picking up handfuls of sand and then letting the sand run through her fingers. "What is Aunt Pat mixed up in?" she said at last.

"We don't know," said Jupe, "but it could be something very nasty."

The Golden Cobra

10

Allie appeared at the salvage yard early the next morning, looking as if she had not slept at all. The Three Investigators were waiting for her near the office in the yard.

"Aunt Pat is crying," she reported. "Ariel is sleeping, just for a change. Bentley is washing the windows."

"And Aunt Mathilda is washing the breakfast dishes," said Jupe, "so you can use the telephone in the office to call the jewelers."

Allie didn't hesitate. She settled herself at the desk in the office, dialed Van Storen and Chatsworth, and gave an excellent imitation of Miss Patricia Osborne asking when the Empress Eugénie necklace would be ready. She listened for a few moments, then said, "Very good. Thank you," and hung up.

"They have the necklace," she told the boys. "They said it will take several days, and they'll hold it until they're notified to deliver it. What a relief!"

"Then it's safe," said Jupiter, "and whatever your new houseman is, he isn't a jewel thief. Now to find out whether a serpent figured in Mrs. Compton's life in any way yesterday."

"You don't suppose Ariel planted a snake in Mrs. Compton's car, do you?" asked Pete.

Allie shuddered.

"That would be enough to cause almost anyone to drive into a bridge abutment," said Jupiter Jones. "However, we shall see."

"What are you going to do?" asked Allie.

"I'm going to the library to look up serpents and demons and strange cults," reported Bob.

"Pete and I will go to the hospital to see Mrs. Compton," Jupiter told Allie. "Hans is taking the small truck into Los Angeles, and we can ride with him."

Allie got up and went to the door of the office. "I'll go home and keep an eye on everyone there," she said.

"We'll call you," promised Jupiter.

She nodded and went out, and Hans rattled up to the door of the office in the truck. "Ready?" he called.

Jupe and Pete climbed into the cab of the truck next to Hans. On the drive into Los Angeles they were silent, each thinking his own thoughts. When they reached Vermont Boulevard, Jupe asked Hans to stop outside a small flower shop. He bought an African violet with several blooms and wrote a card to go with the plant. Hans then drove the boys to Angel of Mercy Hospital.

Outside the hospital, Hans stopped the truck. "You want me to wait?" he said. "What you doing, anyway?"

"We need to talk to a lady about a snake," said Pete.

Hans gulped.

"Never mind, Hans," said Pete. "Don't ask any questions. You'll be happier if you never know."

Jupe got out of the cab. "I think I'd better do this alone," he said. "We don't want to attract too much attention."

"Okay," said Pete. "I'll wait with Hans."

Jupe went up the steps into the hospital carrying his plant.

"Mrs. Margaret Compton?" said Jupiter to the woman at the reception desk. "Is she receiving visitors?"

The woman fingered her way through a box of file cards. "Room 203, East Wing," she said. "The elevator's down the corridor and to your right."

Jupiter thanked her, carried his African violet down the corridor and rode up one floor in the elevator. The elevator opened in front of the nurses' station, a bustle of activity with a doctor making a telephone call, an aide depositing a tray loaded with tiny glasses, and a nurse who ignored Jupiter.

Jupiter cleared his throat. "Mrs. Margaret Compton, Room 203," he said. "Is she able to have visitors?"

The nurse looked up from her charts. "She's just had a sedative," she said sternly.

"Oh." Jupiter Jones allowed his round, cheerful face to droop. "I could come back," he said in a woebegone tone, "but I'd like to see Aunt Margaret and I'm supposed to work this afternoon. They take it out of your pay if you don't show up on time at the drugstore."

"Oh, all right! Just wait a second. Let me check and see if she's okay."

The nurse strode down the hall with a rustle of nylon skirt. She was back in half a minute. "She's awake. You can go in, but don't stay too long. She needs to get some sleep."

Jupe assured her that he would not stay long, and hurried down the hall to Room 203. The door stood open. In the single bed inside was a woman with a round, ruddy face, sleepy eyes and a quantity of white hair. She was firmly anchored by a cast which bulked high under the covers and reached from her foot to her waist.

"Mrs. Compton?" said Jupiter Jones.

The gray, heavy-lidded eyes fell on the African violet in Jupe's hands. "How nice," said the woman.

"It's an especially fine violet," Jupe told her. "It's from the Western Flower Mart, and the customer who purchased it was anxious that it be delivered directly to you."

The woman reached under her pillow and drew out a case with eyeglasses, which she put on. "The card," she said. "Hand me the card, please."

Jupiter put the plant on the table beside the bed and handed the card to her. She squinted at it, managed to focus and read, "With best wishes for your quick recovery." She looked puzzled and turned the card over. "It's not signed," she said.

Jupiter knew this perfectly well.

"Like that thing yesterday," said Margaret Compton. "There was a card on that, too, and it wasn't signed. So careless, not signing cards."

"Perhaps I can help," said Jupiter Jones. "The man who bought the plant was tall and very thin. He had black hair and he was very pale."

"Hmmn," said Mrs. Compton. She seemed on the point of going to sleep.

Jupiter cast about in his mind for some way to introduce serpents into the conversation. Suddenly Margaret Compton roused herself slightly. "Funny! The man who delivered the cobra thing yesterday looked like that. Wonder who . . . who . . . ?"

"Cobra thing?" echoed Jupiter Jones.

"Yes. Nice little . . . nice . . ."

Again Mrs. Compton looked as if she might go to sleep. Jupiter spoke up quickly. "A cobra? How unusual. Do you collect reptiles?"

The gray eyes opened. "No, no! Not really a cobra! It

was a bracelet. I don't usually like . . ." She drifted off for a second.

"You don't usually like snake objects?" prompted Jupe.

"No. Awful things, snakes. Only this was kind of . . . kind of pretty. I put it on. Wish I knew who sent it." The woman's hand reached toward the drawer in the bedside table. "Show you," she murmured. "In my purse."

Jupiter opened the drawer and handed her the small handbag that he found inside. She fumbled with the clasp, got the bag open and groped inside. "Look. Isn't that . . . ?"

"Very interesting," said Jupiter Jones. He took the bracelet and turned it in his hand. It was indeed interesting—a circlet of gold-colored metal with an opening that would allow the wearer to slip it over her wrist. Next to the opening, the gilded band was decorated with the head of a cobra. Tiny specks of precious or semi-precious stones were set into the eyes of the snake. Behind the head the metal band flattened out into the cobra's hood, which was delicately ornamented with green and blue enamel.

Jupiter ran his finger around the inside of the bracelet. It was perfectly smooth. "You had it with you yesterday when you were driving your car?"

"Yes. Wearing it. Was it yesterday? It seems so long now." She turned her head, her eyes closing. "Stupid thing," she complained. "Wheel coming off like that!"

"A wheel came off the car," said Jupiter. "Nothing else disturbed you? Nothing in the car?"

She opened her eyes again. "Nothing in the car? No. But the wheel. It came off. I saw it rolling ahead on the freeway and then, the bridge and…and…"

There was a rustle in the doorway behind Jupe. He turned to see the nurse glaring at him.

"I'm going," he told the nurse. He handed the bracelet

back to Mrs. Compton. "I hope you'll enjoy your plant," he said softly, and he left the room.

"I told you not to stay long," scolded the nurse.

"I'm sorry," said Jupiter. "I only wanted to talk with her for a minute."

He went down the corridor to the elevator, rode back to the first floor and hurried out of the hospital.

"Any luck?" asked Pete when Jupe reached the truck. "Was she any help?"

"She was a great deal of help." Jupe climbed into the truck next to Pete. "She had the serpent with her."

"A snake?" Hans was astonished. "You mean she got a snake with her in hospital?"

"Not a real snake, Hans," said Jupiter. "It was a bracelet with a cobra's head on it."

"Maybe there's some kind of trick," suggested Pete. "The Borgias had rings with secret compartments for poison, and a needle would shoot out and stab the enemy."

Jupiter shook his head. "I examined it closely. There are no gimmicks. It is only a bracelet, but Hugo Ariel delivered it to her personally. Aside from that bracelet, there were no snakes in Mrs. Compton's car when it crashed yesterday. A wheel came off and the car hit an overpass. Now if anyone can tell me how a bracelet can cause a wheel to come off a car, I will cheerfully eat those cast-iron stoves Uncle Titus just bought!"

Bentley's Secret Papers

11

When Jupe and Pete returned to the salvage yard and entered Jupe's workshop, the light over the printing press was flashing. This signaled that the telephone was ringing in Headquarters.

"That may be Allie," said Jupe. "I gave her our private number."

Pete pulled aside the grating that concealed Tunnel Two and scrambled through the corrugated pipe to Headquarters. When Jupe followed him and climbed up through the trap door into the trailer, he was already on the telephone.

"She did have a serpent, but it's only a bracelet," Pete was saying. "It couldn't have hurt her."

Pete listened. Allie's voice came to Jupe as an excited chatter.

"The wheel came off her car," said Pete. "That's all there was to it. It was an accident."

Allie was silent for a few seconds, but then she said something that caused Pete to scowl. "But we just got back!" he protested.

The telephone chattered again, at some length. Pete

sighed and pulled a pad toward himself and wrote an address on it. Finally he said, "All right. After dinner," and hung up.

"What now?" asked Jupiter Jones.

"Allie was calling from the kitchen phone," said Pete. "She said Ariel and her aunt are locked up in the library and Bentley is doing some marketing. Bentley gave her letters of reference. One was from a woman in Brentwood who had to leave town when her husband was transferred to Kansas City, and the other was from a professor in Arcadia. She tried to call Kansas City and there's no listing for the woman. She tried to call the professor in Arcadia. His telephone has been disconnected."

"Not reassuring," said Jupe. "She should have checked on Bentley before she hired him."

"Well she didn't, and now she wants us to do it," said Pete. "She told Bentley she needed to file a form with the Social Security people so she could pay Social Security tax on his salary, and he gave her his home address. It's 1854 North Tennyson in Santa Monica. She wants us to go there right now and find out if Bentley really has a place there and any other stray information we can dig up."

"And you told her we'd go after dinner?" said Jupe.

"Darn right. If I don't show up at home soon, my mother's going to brain me!"

"Aunt Mathilda is also becoming a bit impatient," said Jupiter. "I think you're right. After dinner would be the best time to go to Santa Monica."

"Allie says frog and we jump," observed Pete.

"She *is* our client," Jupiter pointed out. "She shouldn't have hired Bentley on a whim, but she did. Now she wants to know more about him. I think she should. I'll call Bob and ask him to meet us on the highway in front of the market at seven. Is that okay with you?"

"I can make it," said Pete.

"Then seven it is," said Jupiter.

And at seven, The Three Investigators were riding their bikes down the Coast Highway toward Santa Monica. North Tennyson Place, when they located it with the aid of a street map, turned out to be a small court opening off Eleventh. At 1856 there was a large stucco house with a red tile roof. A sign on the lawn indicated that number 1854, the address which Allie had given Pete, was in the rear.

"A garage apartment," decided Jupiter. He went a short way down the drive, then returned, nodding. "An upstairs apartment over a double garage."

"So how do we find out if Bentley really lives there?" asked Pete. "He's at the Jamison house now."

"We ask for him at the big house," said Jupiter. "We could be—let's see—we could be friends of his nephew Freddie. We just rode over from Westwood and decided to drop in on him."

"That's enough to get a conversation started," said Bob.

Jupiter marched to the front door of the stucco house and rang the bell. He waited for almost a minute, then rang again. No one came to the door.

"So much for that great idea," said Pete.

Jupiter picked up his bike, wheeled it to the driveway and looked back at the garage. "Let's assume that Bentley does live here," he said. "It's often possible to tell a great deal about a person simply by observing the place he has chosen for his home."

"So we snoop?" said Pete.

"We can look in the window," replied Jupiter.

Looking in the window of the garage apartment proved to be extremely easy. A flight of stairs went up the outside of the garage and ended in a small landing. There, next to the door of the apartment, was a window with the blinds up.

"How fortunate." Jupiter Jones pressed his nose against the glass.

Pete crowded in beside him and looked, too, and Bob stood on tiptoe to peer over Pete's shoulder.

The last light of the setting sun gleamed in through a window in front of the apartment. It fell on the opposite wall, where there were shelves crammed with books. The boys could see a work table stacked with file folders and more books, a typewriter on a smaller table, a swivel chair and a floor lamp. There was also a studio couch covered with a tan corduroy spread.

"Looks more like an office than a home," said Pete.

Jupiter stepped back from the window. "Our mysterious houseman likes to read," he decided. "He also likes to write."

Bob whistled. "Get a load of those titles!" he said. "The books on the table. He's got *Witchcraft, Folk Medicine and Magic*. That's a new one. We got it at the library this week and it cost $10.95. He's also got *Voodoo–Ritual and Reality*."

"Anything on snakes?" asked Pete.

Jupe tried the doorknob, which wouldn't turn. He then examined the window. "It's not locked," he announced. He looked at his two friends. Pete scanned the empty yard around the garage and Bob stared across at the stucco house.

"We get creamed if we get caught," said Pete.

"We mustn't get caught." Jupe pushed the window sash up. The window opened almost without noise. A second later, Jupe was inside the apartment, with Bob and Pete close behind him.

In addition to the books on magic that Bob had spotted

on the table, the boys saw shelves loaded with accounts of the rituals of primitive peoples, learned tomes on folklore and several works on black magic as it is practiced in modern cities.

"That guy must feel right at home with Aunt Pat Osborne and Hugo Ariel," said Pete.

"If he's read all these books, he's got my respect," said Bob. "I got into some of them today, and they can be tough going."

"An authority on the occult," said Jupe. "One wouldn't expect to find an authority on the occult acting as a houseman."

Jupiter bent over the work table and began to read the tags on the files that were piled there. There was a file called "Mara's Clients," and one marked "The Green Triangle." There was also a file—a thick one—tagged "The Fellowship of the Lower Circle."

"Now I wonder if that could be *our* fellowship." Jupe opened the file. "Oh, yes!" he said.

"What is it?" asked Bob.

Jupe picked up two sheets of paper. "Here is a set of notes on Miss Patricia Osborne. Bentley finds her interesting. For instance, he indicates on this sheet that she has belonged to more than five unusual sects in the past ten years, that she subscribes to two astrology magazines, and that she once traveled to India to study under a philosopher there. The Indian trip didn't last long. Miss Osborne did not find the plumbing adequate. There is also a note here that Miss Osborne moved to the house in Rocky Beach in May, and that Hugo Ariel arrived not long ago."

"Anything else?" asked Pete.

Jupiter pulled out another sheet of paper. "Here's a report from a credit bureau," he said. "It lists Miss Osborne's assets, which are adequate. She would not be considered wealthy."

"Bentley is interested in money?" asked Pete.

Jupiter turned over other papers in the file. "It seems so. There's a similar report on Noxworth, the man who owns a delicatessen. He also owns property in East Los Angeles. He's worth a lot more than his appearance indicates."

"The lady in orange?" asked Pete.

"Madelyn Enderby, the hairdresser?" Jupe thumbed through the file. "She has belonged to a number of odd associations. She owns her own business and her income runs to five figures a year. She has an active account with a stockbroker in the San Fernando Valley."

"Anyone else we know?" asked Bob.

"The lady with the health food shop," said Jupe. "Health food must be quite lucrative. She has applied for a loan to open a second shop in another location. And there are a number of reports here on people we don't know."

"Magic and witchcraft." Bob touched the books on the table. "And also money."

"Perhaps they all go together," said Jupe.

Pete slid open a drawer in the table. It was empty except for a few paper clips and a miniature tape recorder. There was a tape on the take-up spool of the recorder. "I wouldn't mind having that," said Pete. "You could carry it in your pocket."

Bob picked up the instrument. "Nice," he said. "Runs on batteries. No wires to plug in." He pressed a button on one end of the recorder, and a little compartment opened. Inside was a tiny microphone. "Perfect," said Bob. "A little recorder that can be hidden anywhere, with a sensitive microphone. The Secret Service probably doesn't have anything better."

"I wonder what's on that tape," said Jupiter. "How does the rewind mechanism work?"

Bob fumbled with the recorder for a second and watched the tape rewind. Then he reversed the switch. The recorder gave out a few preliminary cracks and rustles, and then The Three Investigators heard someone say, "We can begin."

"That's Ariel's voice!" exclaimed Bob.

"We are not the full fellowship tonight," the voice continued on the recorder. "It may be that we can do nothing. Or it may be that Dr. Shaitan will send us his spirits. The voice of the serpent may speak to us across the miles."

"He bugged Allie's house!" said Pete.

"Must have hidden this near the dining-room door," deduced Bob.

The boys heard the hoarse voice of Madelyn Enderby and the grumbling complaint of Noxworth, the delicatessen man. They heard again Pat Osborne's wish that Margaret Compton be called away.

Then, frightfully clear in the quiet of that small room, they heard the sound. They heard the singing which had frightened Marie out of the Jamison house, and which had driven Allie to ask for help.

"The voice of the serpent," said Jupe.

Bob shuddered and put the tape recorder quickly down on the table, but the dreadful, wordless song went on and on.

The tape turned slowly to its end. The terrible singing faded to a low sob and died. When the little machine emitted only a soft hum, Jupiter Jones realized that he felt cold. The sunlight that had streamed into the apartment was gone, and it was growing dark.

And there was a man standing in the doorway. Bentley!

The Houseman's Sudden Move

12

"Oh my gosh!" exclaimed Pete.

Bob jumped, and quickly turned off the little tape recorder.

Jupiter Jones stood still and considered several possible explanations that he could offer Bentley. He decided that none would do. "We were just leaving," he said.

The man with the walrus mustache remained in the doorway. "Were you planning to go out the way you came in?" he asked. "You used the window, didn't you?" Bentley's voice was angry. There was no bluster in it, and no fright. Jupe saw that Bentley was no longer the meek houseman. It might take dynamite to move him out of the doorway.

Jupiter thought quickly. "Bob," he said, "give me that tape."

Bob lifted the spool of tape off the little recorder and handed it to Jupe.

"That tape is my property!" said Bentley.

Jupe held up the tape. "Tell us, Bentley, how did you record this? Did you hide the machine on the patio the night Miss Osborne had guests?"

The houseman moved then. He lunged across the darkening room and gripped Jupe's wrist.

"Run for it!" shouted Jupe to his friends.

Bob and Pete rushed for the open door. Jupe let go of the tape suddenly and hooked his right leg behind Bentley's left knee.

The houseman floundered backward, cursing. The spool of tape flew across the room. Jupe let it go and ran.

As Jupe shot out the door, Bentley grabbed the back of his shirt. Jupe tore free and bounded down the stairs.

Bentley didn't try to follow. He stood on the landing holding a piece of Jupe's shirt and watched the boys snatch up their bikes and pedal rapidly away.

The Three Investigators were blocks from Tennyson Place before they stopped.

"Are we in trouble, or is Bentley?" wondered Pete. "If he calls the police, we can tell them about that tape and those files."

"The tape and the files can easily be hidden or destroyed," Jupe pointed out. "We *are* guilty of housebreaking, and Bentley has seen us with Allie. He knows where to find us if he wants to."

"What do we do now?" asked Bob.

"We go back to the salvage yard, report to our client and wait. We may not have any trouble. We know that Bentley had to be trespassing on the Jamison property to get that recording of the meeting with Ariel and the others. We know that he has a credit report on Miss Osborne. Wouldn't it be embarrassing if Bentley had to explain why he has that credit report?"

"Blackmail?" asked Pete.

"Possibly," admitted Jupe. "Let's get back to Headquarters and call Allie."

"She could have warned us that Bentley would be at that apartment tonight," said Pete bitterly.

"She may not have known," said Jupe.

At Headquarters, Jupe's guess was proved correct. The telephone was ringing when the boys made their way up through the trap door into the mobile home trailer. The caller was Allie Jamison.

"Oh, you guys, I'm sorry!" she began. Jupiter put the telephone down on a loudspeaker system he had rigged up so that the other Investigators could hear the conversation.

"Bentley caught us," said Jupiter tersely.

"I'm sorry," she repeated. "I tried to reach you, but you'd already left. He said he'd forgotten something he needed. I couldn't tell him he had to stay in nights, could I?"

"I wish you had tried," Jupiter told her. "I am out half a shirt and he now knows we are spying on him. You may be out one houseman."

"You don't think he'll come back here?"

Jupe hesitated. "He might be brazen enough to try," he told Allie, "but we got into his apartment and we saw enough to make us suspect that Bentley might be trying to blackmail your aunt. He has a credit report on her. Also, it was Bentley who was hiding in the garage the night your aunt and Ariel met with the members of the fellowship. He has a tape recording of that meeting."

"That doesn't figure," said Allie. "You couldn't blackmail Aunt Pat. She's clean."

"If she's clean, why is she so upset about Mrs. Compton's accident?"

Allie didn't answer.

"Where is your aunt, by the way?" asked Jupe.

"She's upstairs crying."

"And Hugo Ariel?"

"He's in the library, doing whatever he does."

"Have you heard that singing again?"

"No. It's peaceful as a tomb here, and just about as cheery," said Allie.

"Well, keep your eyes open," called Pete, "and let us know if Bentley shows up."

But Bentley did not show up. Allie called the Jones house first thing in the morning to report the nonappearance of her houseman. Later in the day, Jupiter and Bob rode down to Santa Monica, to Tennyson Place. The windows in the little building behind the stucco house looked blank, and again Jupe rang the bell at the main house. A wispy woman answered the door and told Jupe that it would not be possible for him to deliver a prescription from the drugstore to her tenant in the garage, since he was no longer there. He had moved out that morning and had left no forwarding address.

"Do you recall what moving company he used?" asked Jupe. "There's an unpaid bill at the store."

"He moved himself," said the woman. "He went someplace and got a car and a trailer and moved himself. He didn't have that much to move."

Jupe thanked her and rejoined Bob on the sidewalk. "I think we'll hear nothing at present from Bentley," he told Bob. "I don't know whether I'm glad or sorry."

The Empress Diamonds

13

"I'm beginning to miss Bentley," Allie told Jupiter on the third day after the houseman's disappearance. "He at least moved around. Aunt Pat sits in her room and broods, or she sits on the patio and broods. Ariel hovers. He hardly lets her out of his sight."

"Is he hovering this morning?"

"No. He's having his hair cut."

"What do they talk about?" asked Jupe. He and Allie were leaning on the fence in back of the Jamison house, watching Allie's horse.

"They don't."

"I'm afraid your aunt is involved in something sinister," said Jupe. "Bob has been researching witchcraft, and many of the things your aunt has been doing are mentioned in the witchcraft books. Drawing a circle around her bed with a knife is one. There are also many formulas for invoking spirits or casting spells which involve lighted candles."

"We haven't lit any candles for days," said Allie.

"The auction of the Castillo estate takes place next

week," Jupiter told her. "Does your aunt plan to attend? Mrs. Compton won't be there to bid on that crystal ball."

"No, Mrs. Compton won't go anyplace for months. Her leg was broken in two places. But I don't think Aunt Pat plans anything," said Allie. "She's numb. The only thing she does is call the hospital every day to check and see how Mrs. Compton is doing, and even then she doesn't talk to Mrs. Compton. She talks to the nurse."

Allie looked toward the front of the house. A black limousine had pulled into the drive. A chauffeur got out and opened the back door, and an elegant man dressed in striped trousers and a morning coat emerged from the car holding a package in his gloved hands. Jupe goggled. Such glory was seldom seen in Rocky Beach, and never at eleven in the morning.

Allie's eyes narrowed. "Van Storen and Chatsworth!" she announced. "Everything they do is a major production. They can't make a plain old delivery. I think my mother's necklace is home again. Suppose we meander inside and watch what happens?"

Jupe followed her in through the kitchen. Aunt Pat Osborne was in the hall in the act of accepting the package from the messenger. Jupe noticed that her purple gown was wrinkled and slightly soiled, as if she had worn it for several days—or as if she had given up thinking about what she wore. Her hands shook slightly as she handed a receipt to the man from Van Storen and Chatsworth.

"Allie dear!" she cried, and her voice was high and a bit shrill. "Jupiter. Good morning!"

The jewelers' man departed for his car.

"Your mother's necklace, dear," said Miss Osborne to Allie. "Open the package, won't you, and see if they did a good job?"

Allie silently tore away white wrappings and opened a

dark green leather box. Inside, arranged on white satin, was a necklace that was inches wide. It held more than a hundred diamonds, all blazing with cold, white light.

"Gaudy, isn't it?" said Allie to Jupe.

"My dear, it's most historic," Aunt Pat said.

"It is also heavy as lead," Allie told her. "My mother practically gets a neck ache every time she wears it." She closed the box. "I like pearls better. You don't need an armed guard following you around when you wear them."

Miss Osborne turned away from Allie. "Is that a car in the drive?" she asked.

"It's the werewolf of Rocky Beach, returning from the barber," Allie told her.

"Allie, put the necklace in your mother's safe," said Miss Osborne quickly.

A car door slammed in the back court. Aunt Pat looked toward the rear of the house, and she hid her hands in the folds of her robe. "Right away, dear."

"Okay, Aunt Pat," said Allie. She went up the stairs with the box and just missed Hugo Ariel, who came in reeking of hair tonic.

Allie, without the box, reappeared at the top of the stairs. "I'll talk to you later, huh?" she called down to Jupiter.

"I'll be waiting," promised Jupe, and he left.

Jupiter busied himself in the salvage yard for the rest of the day. He was never far from his workshop, however, where he could check to see if the telephone in Headquarters was ringing. At five, Allie called.

"What did you think of Aunt Pat's performance this morning?" asked Allie.

"I thought it was almost professional," said Jupe. "But it was clear she didn't want Hugo Ariel to know that the necklace was delivered today."

"She must have called the jewelers after Ariel made his

appointment with the barber," said Allie. "I think the delivery was timed so that Ariel wouldn't be there to see it. But if it's so blasted important to keep Ariel away from that necklace, why did Aunt Pat have it returned? She could have ordered Van Storen and Chatsworth to hold it until my mother got home."

"Unless she needs it," said Jupiter.

"She'd better *not* need it!" cried Allie. "It's my mother's."

"True," said Jupiter. "And since it is your mother's, and since you do know the combination of the wall safe, it would be no trouble for you to remove the necklace. Would you let The Three Investigators have it for a short time? There's something I'd like to confirm. Could you get the necklace out of the house without its being seen?"

Allie didn't hesitate. "I've got a poncho that I wear sometimes when I'm riding. You could almost hide a live rooster under that."

"Very good," said Jupiter. "Bring the necklace to the salvage yard the first minute you can. It's probably going to be safer here, anyway. I'll wait for you in my workshop. Now, if you'll hang up, I'll call our friend Worthington. We'll need him tomorrow."

Allie was at the salvage yard before six with the green leather box containing the necklace. Jupe took it from her, and after she left he stowed it away in the desk in Headquarters. Early in the morning Worthington appeared with the Rolls-Royce.

"This is a great responsibility, Master Jupiter," said Worthington, when Jupe gave him the box. "A necklace that once belonged to an empress!"

"You're the only one who can do it," Jupe told him. "It would look very peculiar if I tried, or if Bob or Pete had the necklace."

Worthington nodded. "I'll be extremely careful," he promised. "I should be back here by about two."

"We'll all be waiting," promised Jupe.

It was almost exactly two when Worthington returned to the salvage yard. Jupe met him at the gate and led him to the workshop. Bob and Pete were waiting there with Allie, who sat hunched on an upended crate.

"Miss Jamison," said Worthington, and he sat down in Jupiter's chair. Opening the green leather box, he took out the necklace and draped it across one knee. "It's beautiful," he said, "but it's worthless."

"Worthless!" Allie jumped up. "It's my mother's necklace! It belonged to the Empress Eugénie. It's priceless!"

Worthington was distressed. "I'm sorry, Miss Jamison, but it is *not* the Empress Eugénie necklace. It's an imitation. I called upon three appraisers, saying that I found the necklace among the effects of a recently deceased relative. I was told not to try to obtain insurance on it, since one does not insure costume jewelry."

"Costume jewelry?" Allie looked ready to choke. "Give it to me!"

Worthington handed the necklace over.

"Are you going to discuss this with your aunt?" asked Jupiter mildly.

"Discuss it with her? I'm going home and ram this junk down her throat, and then I'm going to make her tell what she did with the real necklace."

"We can guess what she did with it," said Jupe. "You yourself suggested the safest course. She had an imitation made by Van Storen and Chatsworth, and she directed that the real necklace remain with the jewelers until your parents return."

Allie sat down again on the crate. "That's like finding out that the class dunce is really Albert Einstein. So the necklace is safe."

"But why would she have an imitation necklace made?" asked Pete. "What's she going to do with it?"

Allie frowned. "All this hocus-pocus must have something to do with Ariel. Aunt Pat has been so careful not to let him see the necklace."

"Maybe she's afraid he'll steal it?" guessed Bob.

"Fine! Let him! He can steal this fake and get lost!"

"I don't think this is a simple matter of theft," said Jupiter. "Somehow this necklace business is all mixed up with Mrs. Compton's accident and the fellowship and the power of the singing serpent."

"Is that serpent still singing at your house?" Bob asked Allie.

"No," said Allie. "No one sings at our house."

"Scared?" asked Pete.

"Yes, a little."

"I don't think you're in any danger," Jupiter told her. "As long as Ariel doesn't suspect you of being a threat to him, he won't bother you. Bentley is involved in some way and may show up again, but he doesn't seem violent."

"It isn't me I'm scared for," said Allie. "Why should I be scared for me? They think I'm only a pesky kid. I'm scared for Aunt Pat. Tonight she and Ariel are going to another meeting of that creepy fellowship. I heard them talking about it this morning. Ariel said Dr. Shaitan was assembling the others at Torrente Canyon and Aunt Pat had to go. She doesn't want to. She cried a lot. But she's going."

"Excellent!" said Jupiter.

"It isn't excellent!" shouted Allie. "It's horrible. I hate to see her like this."

"I'm afraid that until we discover the secret of the fellowship, you won't see her any other way," said Jupiter. "Worthington, could you . . ."

"I'd be delighted to pay another visit to the house in Torrente Canyon," said Worthington.

"I'm coming, too," announced Allie.

"Allie, please!" said Pete.

"It's *my* aunt," she pointed out. "It's also my mother's necklace that's involved, and Ariel is living in my house. I'm going. Worthington, where will I meet you this evening?"

"I had thought," said Worthington, "that the parking lot in front of the Rocky Beach Market—"

"Fine. What time?"

"Would half-past seven be agreeable, miss?"

"Perfectly. See you at seven-thirty." Allie strode out, hiding the necklace under her poncho.

"A strong-minded young lady," said Worthington.

The Three Investigators didn't disagree.

Dr. Shaitan's Spirits

14

Worthington had no cause to change his mind that evening. Allie was waiting with The Three Investigators when he appeared at the Rocky Beach Market driving his gray Ford. She was calm enough, but her jaw was set in a way that meant she planned to see some action. "I'm going to get into that house," she told Worthington as he held the car door for her.

"Yes, miss," said Worthington.

"We'll get into the house," Jupiter Jones assured her. "We have a plan."

"What is it?"

"Wait and see," advised Jupe.

Allie had a long wait. They reached Torrente Canyon to find the road outside the walled house empty and deserted. "Good!" exclaimed Pete. "We're the first ones here."

Worthington parked up the road beyond the house and Bob got out of the car. "I'll keep watch from that bunch of oleanders across from the gate."

"Good," said Jupe.

Bob nodded and walked back toward the big house. He was hidden in the oleanders, watching, when the first car came up the road.

It was Madelyn Enderby who got out, crossed to the gate and reached for the telephone set into the wall. Bob was about to leave his hiding place when the purple Corvette appeared. Hugo Ariel was at the wheel. In the twilight, Bob could barely see Miss Patricia Osborne. Her head was bowed and she dabbed at her eyes with a handkerchief. Ariel helped her out of the car. The buzzer on the gate rasped, and Ariel and Miss Osborne joined Madelyn Enderby and went in.

A few minutes later, a pale blue Cadillac rolled to a stop. Bob saw a thin, brown-haired man go to the telephone in the wall. Careful not to make a sound, Bob slipped out from behind the oleanders and crossed over to the gate.

The man was holding the telephone receiver to his ear, listening. Then he said, "I will descend to the lower circle."

He hung up and turned.

"Good evening," said Bob. "I'm looking for 1483 Torrente Circle."

"This isn't Torrente Circle," said the man. "It's Torrente Canyon Drive. You're on the wrong street."

The buzzer on the gate sounded. The man stepped past Bob, opened the gate and went through.

Bob returned to Worthington's Ford. "I will descend to the lower circle," he said. "The guy on the phone says, 'The night is dark,' and then you have to answer, 'I will descend to the lower circle.'"

"The password!" Allie leaped from the car.

"Keep alert," Jupe told Worthington.

"I'll be waiting for you," promised the chauffeur.

The Three Investigators followed Allie down the road to the gate. Jupiter lifted the telephone receiver from the niche and put it to his ear.

"The night is dark," said a husky voice.

"I will descend to the lower circle," answered Jupe. His tone was as deep as he could manage.

The telephone clicked and Jupe hung up. A moment later the gate buzzed. Pete turned the handle and pushed, and the huge portal swung easily in.

The Three Investigators and Allie slipped inside. The gate shut behind them. When Bob tried the handle on the inside, it wouldn't move.

"There's a switch hidden in the ivy to the right of the gate," said Pete. "The night I fell off the wall, that thug used it to open the gate before he tossed me out."

Bob peered at the ivy. "I see it. Looks like a circuit breaker."

"Don't touch it," warned Jupe. "It might set off some kind of alarm. We know where it is. We can use it if we need to get out fast."

"Now for the house," said Allie.

"No. Now we wait," Jupe told her. "If this meeting of the fellowship is anything like the one we saw before, there are more people to come."

Jupiter was right. From a shadowy corner of the grounds, the boys and Allie watched the gate open again and again to admit visitors. After fifteen minutes, eight more people had walked up the long drive to the house.

"Eight, plus Madelyn Enderby, Miss Osborne and Ariel and that one I overheard on the telephone, said Bob. "That makes twelve, the same as the other night. I wonder if that's all."

It was. When ten minutes had passed without a sound from the gate, they decided to move.

"Now let's watch it," warned Pete. "I don't want to meet that guy who guards this place."

They moved slowly and noiselessly across the grass. When they were quite close to the house, they saw that one tiny chink of light showed through drapes which had been drawn over a long window. They edged away from this and circled to the back of the building.

"There's a door," said Jupe softly. He crept forward in the darkness, careful not to stumble on an unexpected doorstep. He felt for the doorknob and found it. But the door was locked.

Allie backed away and looked up at the rear of the house. "Up there," she whispered. "A window, and if anything's open anywhere, it's that. It's so high they wouldn't bother with it."

"Probably a pantry or a storeroom," guessed Jupe. He looked at the opening doubtfully. "It's very small."

"I can get through," said Allie quickly.

"No, you can't," put in Bob. "You're not thin enough."

"You are, Bob," said Jupe. "Be careful."

"Don't worry," said Bob.

Pete braced himself against the house, and Bob clambered up onto his shoulders.

"Is it open?" asked Allie.

Jupe shushed her and listened to wood sliding on wood. Bob grunted, pulled himself up, slipped in through the window and disappeared. Perhaps a minute ticked by. Then the lock turned softly on the back door and the door opened.

"Come on," whispered Bob. "They're all out front someplace."

The Investigators and Allie crept across a kitchen, guided by a faint glow from the front of the house. At the kitchen doorway they stopped and looked into a wide hall. To the left they saw a broad staircase, and to the right, opposite the staircase, they saw an arched doorway. The light came from that door.

Jupe drew back into the kitchen. Outside the uncurtained windows, the moon shone dimly through the treetops. Jupe could barely make out the shape of a stove. He heard a faucet drip, and he saw that there was a second door leading out of the kitchen. It showed as a black, gaping hole in the wall, to the left of the first door.

Jupe tapped Bob and pointed. Bob nodded. Jupe took Allie's arm and guided her through the second door into inky blackness. Pete and Bob followed.

They had to feel their way. They went forward, inch by inch. Strange objects got in their path. Pete touched one and felt velvet. It was a sofa.

At last there was a hairline of light. It had to be coming through a crack under a door. Jupe let go of Allie's arm, took two slow steps forward and let his fingers slide over wooden panels until he touched a knob. It turned without a sound. Jupe pulled the knob toward him and opened the door a few inches.

He was looking out across the broad hall and in through the lighted archway.

"The fellowship is assembled," said a familiar voice from across the hall. Hugo Ariel was speaking.

Jupe opened the door a few more inches, and the others crowded around him. They stared into a chamber where tall, black candles burned in silver candlesticks. In the middle of the room was a large, round table, covered with a black cloth. Twelve people were grouped around it, standing behind chairs. Hugo Ariel seemed to be at the head of the table, facing the hall. Before him was a chair that looked more like a throne. Gilded wooden cobras twisted around the arms and up over the back of the thing. Next to it stood Pat Osborne, looking forlorn.

The fellowship waited, not moving, in a room that seemed filled with motion. Jupe realized that the group was surrounded by a shifting, billowing darkness. Black hangings covered walls and windows and swayed with every draft.

Ariel shifted his weight behind the throne. "The fellowship is assembled," he said again.

The boys and Allie heard footsteps on the stairs. A shape came between them and the candlelit room. Someone wearing a long, black cloak paused in the archway, then swept into the room and went to the far side of the table. He sat down in the serpent throne and, for the first time, Jupiter and the others could really see him. Jupe heard Pete let out a faint gasp.

If Hugo Ariel was pale, this man was ashen. His face was so white that it seemed to glow and float against the blackness of his own garb—for he was swathed from head to toe in the color of night. Even his hair was hidden by a close-fitting black cap.

The man drew his cape around him with gleaming white hands and bowed his head slightly.

The assembled company sat down.

The man on the throne clapped his hands twice. Hugo Ariel glided away from the table, then returned with a tray. On it was a silver cup, which Ariel offered to the man in the chair.

"Belial favor all those here!" said the man. He took the cup and put it to his lips.

"Moloch hear us!" It was a chorus of voices.

The man handed the cup to Pat Osborne. She took it, looking as if she might weep. "Belial favor all those here," she said shakily. She drank and passed the cup as the others intoned the prayer to Moloch.

Again and again the favor of Belial was asked. Again and again the group called upon Moloch to hear them. The cup came back at last to the person in the serpent chair, who returned it to Ariel.

Next Ariel produced a small charcoal brazier with four legs. He put this on the table in front of the caped one, who then stood and extended his hands over the live coals in the thing. "Asmodeus, Abaddon and Eblis, look upon us!" he cried.

Ariel offered a silver dish. The man in black sprinkled something from it onto the brazier. A column of smoke sprang up and a thick, sweet smell drifted to the watchers across the hall.

"Belial hear us!" pleaded the caped man. "Send the power of the serpent to guard us. Let us see your countenance. Let us hear your voice!"

The man was still then. Everyone was still, and in that stillness Allie and the boys heard the beginning of a dreaded sound. Someone or something was singing.

Allie started, as if she wanted to run. Jupe grasped her arm and held her still.

The sound grew louder. It rose, wordless, until it stung at the bone and shriveled the flesh.

Again the man in the cape dipped into the dish. Again incense was thrown into the brazier. And in the seething mass of smoke, something moved!

Bob took a sudden, deep breath.

"Belial has favored us!" proclaimed the caped man. "The serpent that never dies is among us!"

The silent watchers trembled when they saw the thing that writhed in the smoke. It was a huge cobra, a shimmer of green and blue, a spread of hood, a red-eyed glitter.

The song went on and on until it was a fearful, shrill pulse of noise that made Jupe want to cover his ears. At last, mercifully, it began to dwindle. The smoke thinned. The terrible serpent paled and faded. The singing ceased. The thing was gone.

The caped man seated himself. "The good of one of our fellowship is the good of all," he said. "We will join hands."

Pat Osborne stared straight ahead, but she put her hand on the table. The man in black took it.

Jupiter nudged Pete. Footsteps came softly down the stairs, and a dark shape blocked the watchers' view of the fellowship. It was the muscular man who had been patrolling the grounds the night Pete fell off the wall. He stood in the hall, surveying the room where the caped man presided over his brazier and his disciples. After a moment, he went into the ritual room, walked to the far side of the table and bent to whisper into the ear of the man on the throne.

"Impossible!" said the caped man. "We are all present."

"There should be thirteen," insisted the other. "Miss Enderby, Mr. Ariel and Miss Osborne came in together. Everyone else came separately. But I opened the gate eleven times. There should be a thirteenth member!"

The man in the cape stood up. "It seems that we may have an intruder nearby," he told his followers. "The fellowship is dismissed. I will summon you again when the time is right."

The Investigators drew back from the door, and Jupiter closed it silently.

"They're on to us," whispered Pete.

There was a scraping of chairs from the ritual room, and a babble of voices.

"Very thorough," said Jupiter softly. "That man who tends the gate can count."

"Let's go!" urged Bob. "In two seconds they'll be searching this place."

"You go," said Jupiter Jones.

"You're kidding!"

"I'm not." Jupiter's voice was so low that the others could scarcely hear him over the bustle of the departing fellowship. "Go out the back, the way we came in. Make a disturbance. Climb the wall. Set off the alarm. Make them think they've scared everybody off. Then get to the car and tell Worthington I'll meet you at Sunset and Torrente as soon as I can."

"Okay, Jupe, but watch it," said Bob.

"I will," promised Jupiter.

He heard his friends slip back to the kitchen. Then the kitchen door opened and slammed shut. He heard shouts from the grounds outside. Allie yelled, and he heard the clamor of the alarm bell. Floodlights blazed in the yard, and from the road came the sound of cars starting.

Jupe waited. Soon there was quiet—the quiet of an empty house. Jupiter opened the door, looked around the hall, then hurried across to the ritual room, where he hid behind the black drapes. After a time there were steps on the drive outside. The inhabitants of the house on Torrente Canyon came into the hall and closed the door.

"Just kids," said one voice. "Kids get curious."

"You have to hand it to them, Max," said a second voice. It was the voice of the man who had occupied the throne. "They sure moved going over that wall."

Jupiter Jones smiled to himself. Bob, Pete and Allie had gotten clean away—and he now intended to find out whatever he could!

The High Priest's Scheme

15

Jupiter found a small tear in the black hangings that shrouded the ritual room. He stood stock still, so that he would not reveal his presence to the men in the room, but his fingers worked at the little tear, making it bigger. Soon he could look out into the room, and he saw the man named Max touch a switch near the door. An overhead light clicked on.

Jupiter almost sighed. By flickering candlelight, the ritual room had had a dark fascination. Now that fascination was gone. Jupe saw that the covering on the table was dusty, and that the hangings in the room were cheap and sagging. The silver candlesticks were dented and flecked with tarnish.

If the room was shabby, the two men in it were equally worn. The man with the gray hair—the man who had thrown Pete off the grounds—was going from one tall candle to another, snuffing out the flames. Deep lines ran from his eyes down to the corners of his mouth. He was beginning to run to fat, and a double chin drooped over the top of his dark shirt.

His companion lolled on the throne, absently stroking the carved cobra on one of the arms. He had pushed the chair back, the better to put his feet on the table. In the full light, Jupiter saw that his ghastly paleness was not natural. Some greenish, chalky substance was caked in the creases around his mouth and beside his nose.

"That telephone system at the gate is a total bust," said the man in the chair.

The man named Max snuffed out the last of the candles and sat down wearily. "Look," he said, "I could go down and stand at that gate and check everybody who comes through, but that won't work either. You can't fight kids. They'll get in somehow, and they talk. We've made a bundle here. Why don't we fold the operation and move? You can have a fine time being Dr. Shaitan in San Francisco or San Diego or Chicago. Let's go before things hot up for us."

"But Max, the best is yet to come," said the man called Dr. Shaitan. He reached up and pulled off his black cap. Jupe wanted to laugh. The high priest of the sinister fellowship had flaming red hair. An instant later, the black cape was unfastened and thrown aside. The man took a crumpled tissue from his pocket and dabbed at his chalky face. The greenish powder came off in streaks, revealing pink skin.

"Do you have to do that here?" complained Max. "You're getting that stuff all over the place."

"I'm thinking." Dr. Shaitan rolled the stained tissue between his hands. "It's taken us a long time to set up this bunch of pigeons. The Enderby woman came through like clockwork when her landlady went to Dubuque, and old man Robertson made a beautiful donation when the power of the singing serpent was invoked to keep that building contractor from putting up a high rise next to his house. Pat Osborne hasn't paid off yet, but she will and it will be juicy. Hugo Ariel will see to it."

"It may be so juicy that we won't be able to handle it," said Max.

"We can handle anything," declared Shaitan. "You just have to know where the market is." He smiled. "Ellis did a good job with the Compton woman. No one suspected a thing. Did you notice Pat Osborne tonight?"

"Scared," said Max.

"Very much so," said Shaitan with grim satisfaction. "She'll be even more scared if she doesn't make her offering. Now Noxworth isn't going to scare easily, but he won't have all these pangs of conscience, either, and he's got real dough. No hot stuff there. We'll get cold, hard cash. We see to it that his competition folds up and he'll be duly grateful. It'll be worth hanging in here for that."

Max snorted. "The things that these nuts get upset about floor me," he declared. "The Osborne dame wants a crystal ball that once belonged to a movie star, and Noxworth can't stand it when the place across the street draws more customers than his own lousy delicatessen. Noxworth's got money he hasn't even counted yet. Why should he care?"

"It isn't the money," said Shaitan. "It's the power. These people want to believe they've got power, so we convince them that they do."

"How are you planning to convince Noxworth?" asked Max. "Is his competition going to have an accident on the freeway, too?"

The man who enjoyed being Dr. Shaitan put his fingertips together and stared at them dreamily. "You lack imagination, Max. No, the singing serpent will perform in a different key for Noxworth. It will be a bit riskier, but it may work. Even if it doesn't, Noxworth won't get off the hook because we'll see to it that he, personally, delivers the serpent. And we'll see to it that he witnesses the result. He'll come through, just the way Pat Osborne will come through."

Dr. Shaitan yawned. "I'm beat," he said. "I'm going to bed." He got up and started for the doorway.

"You left your cape," said Max.

"I'll get it in the morning." Shaitan's footsteps went away up the stairs.

"Slob!" snarled Max. He pushed back his chair and went to the doorway. The light switch clicked and the lower floor of the house on Torrente Canyon went dark. Jupe heard Max follow the high priest of the fellowship up the stairs. A door slammed. Water gurgled in the pipes at the back of the house.

Jupiter slipped out from behind the black drapes and tiptoed out of the ritual room into the hall. He stole to the back of the house, and was pleased to find that Dr. Shaitan and his assistant had neglected to lock the kitchen door after they returned to the house. Jupe slipped out without making a sound and started for the gate. He looked back once to see lights in several of the upper windows. The shadow of a man showed clearly on one drawn shade. Jupiter grinned. Dr. Shaitan had his head thrown back. He was gargling.

Jupe wished he had a photograph of the demonic high priest at his bedtime ritual. Then he was at the wall, searching in the moonlight for the switch hidden in the ivy—the switch that would open the gate and release him. When his fingers touched it, he took a deep breath and flipped the plastic lever. The alarm did not clang. The floodlights did not blaze. There was a faint sound from the house. It might have been something triggered by the switch, but Jupe did not pause to wonder. He stepped to the gate, turned the handle and tugged. The gate opened.

At that, stunningly, the floodlights did glare.

"Hey! Hey, you kid! Hold it right there!"

Jupiter didn't turn around. He didn't have to. He knew instantly that the voice belonged to the muscular Max. He began to run.

"Hold it, I said!" shouted Max.

Something hit Jupiter—something large. He felt himself tumbling over and over, rolling in the road. And someone was rolling with him.

"Keep down, you idiot!" said a voice in his ear.

There was a roar, and buckshot whined overhead and crackled through the oleanders beside the road.

"Don't move," cautioned the person who was holding Jupe down.

Jupiter winced as another roar came from the driveway of the walled house and more shot whistled above him.

"Now!" cried Jupe's captor. He flung himself away from Jupe. Jupe lunged to his feet and saw a man sprint toward the place where Torrente Canyon Road came to a dead end. The man looked back at Jupe for a bare second. "Run!" he shouted.

Jupe ran in the opposite direction. He ran as fast as his trembling legs would carry him.

Worthington's Ford was parked at the corner of Sunset and Torrente, and the motor was running. The back door popped open. "Okay?" asked Bob.

Jupiter scrambled into the car. "Go!" he shouted.

Worthington went so quickly that Jupe was thrown to the floor.

"What happened?" asked Allie from the front seat.

Jupiter pulled himself up. "There was a man outside that gate tonight with a large mustache and fair hair. Does that sound like anyone you know?"

"Bentley?"

"I think so," said Jupe. "I'm almost positive it was Bentley. And I wish I could talk to him now. I'd like to thank him."

"For what?" asked Allie.

"If it hadn't been for Bentley, I might now be punctured in several places. Dr. Shaitan's friend lost his patience with juvenile intruders, and Dr. Shaitan's friend has a double-barreled shotgun."

Trouble for Aunt Pat

16

"It's witchcraft, but it isn't," declared Bob.

The Three Investigators were in Headquarters, reviewing the events of the night before. Bob had his file on the case of the singing serpent. He also had several books. One was *Witchcraft, Folk Medicine and Magic*, the book that the boys had seen in Bentley's apartment. Bob tapped the volume. "Those men are going by the book," he said. "It could be this book, or any book on witchcraft. They're all pretty much the same, whether the author is writing about voodoo in the West Indies or what happens among the aborigines in Australia. It works the same way, only what those guys in Torrente Canyon are doing can't possibly work."

"Because the victim doesn't believe?" asked Jupiter Jones.

"Right. Because the victim doesn't believe."

"You care to explain that?" asked Pete.

"It's simple." Bob held up the book on magic. "This one's by Dr. Henry W. Barrister, who's a professor of anthropology at Ruxton University. He's been to Africa and

South America and Mexico and Australia and he keeps finding about the same thing. When a witch doctor wants to put the whammy on someone, he can use different methods. With voodoo, he sticks pins in a doll. In Mexico, the witch goes to a nice dark cave and lights candles and says spells. Then he cuts a thread. That thread is the victim's life. The witch doctor has cut his life short. Pretty soon the victim learns that his life has been cut, and he gets sick and dies."

"I don't get it."

"The victim believes," put in Jupiter. "He knows a spell has been cast and he believes that he'll die, so he does."

"You mean just believing in a thing like that can hurt you?" Pete looked a bit green.

"If you believe strongly enough," said Bob. Again he tapped the book by the anthropology professor. "The man who wrote this has seen people get sick and die of terror because someone put a curse on them."

"Then Ariel and Shaitan are doing the same thing," decided Pete, "only they're using a serpent. The serpent is delivered and bang! Big trouble for whoever gets the snake."

"That's what has happened," agreed Jupe, "but, as Bob says, it can't be magic. The victims don't believe. Margaret Compton wasn't afraid of the singing serpent. To her, it was only an odd bracelet. It's Allie's aunt who believes that the accident happened because the serpent was delivered to Mrs. Compton. She blames herself and she's afraid. It's natural. She isn't a malicious woman and she wasn't expecting anything so drastic.

"But of course we know that the accident was no accident at all. I heard that much last night. The man who calls himself Shaitan arranged with someone named Ellis for the wheel to come off Mrs. Compton's car."

"And now Shaitan and his pal are dreaming up something to eliminate Noxworth's competition," said Bob gloomily.

Jupiter rubbed his forehead. "It's the place across the street," he said. "Those were the words Max used. The place across the street has more customers than Noxworth."

"Another delicatessen?" said Pete. "That's nuts!"

"It is to us," agreed Jupiter, "but remember, Miss Osborne wanted the crystal ball which had belonged to Ramon Castillo. Miss Enderby had a quarrel with her landlady and invoked the power of the serpent. Some very silly things can stir up strong feelings.

"And there is the desire for power. Shaitan said it—these people want power. Shaitan wants money. I wonder what Bentley wants. He's the big question mark. He goes to work as a houseman, then disappears when his interest in magic and in the fellowship is discovered. What *is* his interest?"

"Maybe it's money, too," said Bob. "Maybe he is a blackmailer. Whatever it is, be glad. He kept you from getting peppered with buckshot."

"I am glad. He must have seen the gun in Max's hands. He jumped on me and knocked me out of the line of fire and kept me down until Max had used up both his charges of shot."

"So he's still the mystery man," said Bob, "but we know what the score is on The Fellowship of the Lower Circle. They're a bunch of con men milking superstitious people like Allie's Aunt Pat. What do we do now?"

"Tell the police?" suggested Pete.

"Would they believe us?" asked Jupe quietly.

"Mrs. Compton *was* hurt," Pete insisted.

"An accident. A wheel comes off a car. Who knows

why? If it was done cleverly enough, it could be impossible to detect. And even if we could persuade the police to visit the house in Torrente Canyon, what would they find? Two men and some black candles. We can't go to the police. Not now, at any rate. We need proof."

"Ariel?" said Bob. "He's putting the screws on Aunt Pat for sure."

"He'd never admit it, and she'd never testify against him," decided Jupe. "She's terrified of him. Whatever the fellowship wants from her, she will eventually give them. She's afraid not to."

"We can all guess what they want," said Pete.

Jupe nodded. "Something that might be too hot to handle, unless you know the right people. They don't want money from Miss Osborne. She hasn't much. They want the Empress Eugénie necklace."

"Which is safe in the vault at the jewelers'," said Bob.

"Jupe! Jupiter, where are you?" The cry came to the boys through the air vent of the mobile home trailer. "Jupiter Jones!"

Jupe leaped up. "That's Allie!"

Pete snatched open the trap door that led to Tunnel Two. "Never a dull moment when that kid's around," he said.

Bob and Jupe followed Pete through Tunnel Two to Jupiter's workshop, then ran toward the driveway of the salvage yard. Allie was there, near the office. She was almost in tears, and there was an ugly red mark on one cheek.

"Dr. Shaitan!" she said. "He's at the house!"

Pete whistled. "Did he do that?" he asked.

"What?" demanded Allie.

"Your face. It looks as if someone hit you."

Allie pushed her hair back with both hands. "Aunt Pat," she said.

"You're kidding! Your aunt socked you?"

"She didn't mean it," said Allie hastily. "She was scared, that's all. She looked out and saw this big car pull up, see, and it was Shaitan with his black cape and his cap and the whole bit. The other creep who lives in that house was dressed as a chauffeur. Aunt Pat told me to get out. I wasn't about to do that, so she hauled off and whammed me a good one and shoved me out the back door just as the front doorbell was ringing. And she locked the door." Allie gave a gasping little laugh. "I didn't know she had it in her."

"*Now* we call the cops!" declared Pete.

"No, we can't. Don't you see? She's alone there with those men. They might hurt her."

"Then we get to your house," said Jupe. "Quickly!"

They raced up the street to the Jamison house, but they were only in time to see a black car pull away. Max was at the wheel and Ariel sat beside him. Shaitan, capped and caped, sat in the rear.

The front door of the house was unlocked. Allie rushed through and let it bang back against the wall. "Aunt Pat!" she shouted.

Miss Osborne was a lavender shadow in the green-gold living room. "Allie? Allie, I'm so sorry. I didn't mean to strike you."

Allie ran toward her aunt. "Are you all right?"

"Yes, I'm all right." A single tear ran down Miss Osborne's cheek and trembled, unnoticed, on her chin. "Mr. Ariel and . . . and . . ."

"Dr. Shaitan?" said Jupiter Jones.

Miss Osborne reached out blindly, touched a chair and sat down.

"Did they want the necklace?" asked Jupiter. "Did you give them the imitation?"

Miss Osborne stared at him, at the other two boys and at Allie. "You knew?"

"We've known for some time that there was an imitation. We guessed that Shaitan wanted the Empress Eugénie diamonds, and that that's why Hugo Ariel stayed in this house. Did they threaten you, Miss Osborne?"

She began to sob. "It was horrible! Horrible! They said I had to make an offering." She took a handkerchief from a pocket in her gown and scrubbed at her eyes. Then she blew her nose in a determined manner.

"But I fooled them," she said proudly. "I pretended to hold out. I made them wait. Wasn't that clever? Because the thing they have is paste, and the real necklace is safe!"

"In the vault at the jewelers'?" asked Jupe.

"At the jewelers'? Why, no. It was delivered when they brought the imitation. The real one was in a sack—an ordinary paper sack. I put it in the pocket of my robe and then later I hid it."

Allie sighed. "It's still in this house?"

"Of course it's in this house. Where else would it be? But it's safe. No one will ever find it. I'll never tell. I won't even tell *you*."

Allie knelt beside her aunt. "All right, Aunt Pat. You don't have to tell me. But we must call the police." Her voice was very gentle.

"No!"

"Now we have proof," said Jupiter. "What they did to you is extortion. You must speak to Chief Reynolds."

"No!"

"Miss Osborne, those are dangerous men, and they are by no means finished with their business in Los Angeles. Unless you talk to the police, innocent people may be hurt."

"An innocent person *has* been hurt, and it's my fault. I

can't! I won't! You don't know what you're asking! You don't know what it would mean!"

"All right, Miss Osborne," said Jupiter. "Only think about this: How long will it take Dr. Shaitan to discover that the necklace is an imitation? What will happen then?"

Pat Osborne was silent.

"Think about it, Miss Osborne," said Jupe, "and don't wait too long."

A Warning from Pete

17

Miss Osborne was still sitting in the living room, dazed, when The Three Investigators left.

"That woman is really, really dumb!" said Pete.

"Is she ever!" agreed Bob. "And we can't do anything if she won't talk to the police."

"There is one thing we can do," said Jupiter. "We know what Shaitan plans. He's going to eliminate the delicatessen that's across the street from Noxworth's store. We'd better locate that delicatessen and warn the owner. He'll be the next one to receive the serpent."

"But will he believe us?" asked Bob.

"Probably not," said Jupiter. "However, we can give him one of our cards and ask him to call us if a serpent object suddenly appears in his life. When the serpent *is* delivered, he'll be curious. I think he will call us."

The boys reached The Jones Salvage Yard and went into the office, where Jupiter consulted the Los Angeles telephone directory. "Noxworth's Mini Market is at Beverly and Third," he said.

"There couldn't be two of them," said Bob. "Do we call Worthington?"

Jupiter frowned. "Let's not run Worthington ragged. We can get into Los Angeles on the bus. Once we see Noxworth's store, we can easily spot the opposition. Only, I have a feeling we'd better not all go. If Shaitan shows up at Allie's house again, she'll call here. I want to be here if that call comes."

Bob leaned against a filing cabinet. "I'd like to stay here, too," he said.

"Okay. I'll go," said Pete. "But if that call comes from Allie, you guys had better yell for Chief Reynolds and the Rocky Beach Police Department. No telling what those crooks will do when they find out the necklace is a fake."

Pete hiked off to the highway then, to catch the bus into Santa Monica. In Santa Monica he transferred to a Los Angeles bus, and by noon he was standing at the corner of Beverly and Third.

Pete spotted Noxworth's Mini Market immediately. It was directly across the street from the bus stop, and Pete decided that the store matched the man. The windows, like Mr. Noxworth's undershirt, would have been better for a good washing. Tatters of newspaper decorated the parking lot, and someone had dropped a pop bottle near the door. Shards of green glass lay there undisturbed.

Pete scanned his side of the street. A television repair shop shared the block with another food store. Gleaming chrome letters on the wall of the delicatessen proclaimed that H. Hendricks supplied gourmet foods. Inside the shop, a large man with dark, curly hair scooped potato salad into a carton, while a plump lady consulted her shopping list. The white formica counter was spotless and uncluttered. There was no other food store in sight.

Satisfied that he had located Noxworth's competition, Pete waited until the plump lady left the store. Then he went in.

"Mr. Hendricks?" said Pete.

"Yes?" said the man behind the counter.

"You *are* Mr. Hendricks?" asked Pete. "I mean, you own this store, don't you?"

The man looked Pete over. Pete saw that he had more than his fair share of muscles. There was no trace of gray in his dark hair, and the brown eyes were steady and clear. In short, Mr. Hendricks looked well able to take care of himself.

"You need a job, son?" he asked. "I hired a boy to deliver for me last week, but if—"

"I don't need a job," said Pete. "I only need to be sure you own this shop."

"You fussy about who sells you your pickles? Okay, I'm Hendricks and I own this place. Now what's on your mind?"

"I came to warn you, Mr. Hendricks. I know this is going to sound crazy, but something bad will happen to you. I don't know exactly what, but it'll be bad."

Pete put one of the cards of The Three Investigators on the counter and wrote the private number of Headquarters on it. After a moment's thought, he added the number of The Jones Salvage Yard.

"If you should see a snake—" began Pete.

"I'll call the zoo," said Hendricks.

"I don't mean that kind of snake," protested Pete. "It won't be a live snake. It might be a statue of a snake, or a pin or something like that. It will be a cobra. If someone delivers a cobra to you, call either of these numbers. If one doesn't answer, the other will."

Hendricks did not touch the card. He looked as if he were waiting for the punch line to a joke.

"We think we can help you," Pete said quickly. "It's

very serious. Someone's out to get you. When you see the snake, you'll know that something bad is going to happen. Now if you'll cooperate with us, we can—"

"Beat it," said Hendricks.

"Mr. Hendricks, we want to help."

"I said beat it!" The brown eyes had gone hard.

"Maybe when you see the snake, you'll change your mind," said Pete.

Hendricks started around the counter and Pete fled to the door. "Call any time," he said.

"Scram!" shouted Hendricks.

Pete scrammed. On the bus ride back to Rocky Beach he decided, unhappily, that he had not been at all successful in delivering the warning. He felt that Jupiter Jones might have done a better job. Jupe could be very convincing.

It was afternoon when Pete reached The Jones Salvage Yard. Bob and Jupe were there. Bob was looking on as Jupe hosed down a sundial which Uncle Titus Jones had recently acquired.

"Noxworth's competition is a man named Hendricks," said Pete. "He is one heck of a tough guy."

"Did you warn him?" asked Bob.

"I warned him, and I left our card and the telephone number of the yard and the telephone number of Headquarters. He chased me out of his store."

"He didn't believe you." Jupiter turned off the hose. "We expected that. But if he does receive a snake object, he may call."

"I don't think we should wait for that call," said Bob. "We should go to the police now. How can we protect a man who won't listen to us?"

Jupiter turned toward the gate of the salvage yard. A

patrol car was pulling in, and Chief Reynolds was at the wheel. "It looks," said Jupe, "as if the police have come to us."

The head of the Rocky Beach Police Department stopped his car and got out. He approached The Three Investigators with the air of a man who is both weary and irritated. "Would you hot-shots please tell me what you're doing now?" he asked.

"Have you had a complaint about us?" asked Jupe.

"I've had a call from the Los Angeles Police Department, Juvenile Division. They asked me if I knew you, and I had to admit that I did." The chief pointed a finger at Pete. "You paid a call on a merchant named Hendricks today," he accused.

Pete gulped.

"You left your calling card and the telephone number of this place," said the chief, "which is why the LAPD called me. They think that you're trying to shake down Mr. Hendricks."

"Shake him down?" cried Pete. "I wasn't trying to shake him down. I was trying to warn him."

"It didn't sound that way to Hendricks. It sounded more like a threat. Care to explain?"

"We'd be glad to," said Jupiter quickly.

"Fine," said Chief Reynolds. "I'm listening."

Jupiter decided that professional ethics would not permit him to mention Allie and her aunt, but otherwise he told the chief everything. He told of finding a mysterious house in Torrente Canyon, and of the peculiar brand of magic being practiced there. He admitted entering the house. He related the conversation he had overheard between Shaitan and his confederate. "We believe that Mr. Hendricks is in danger," he finished. "When the power of the singing serpent is invoked—"

Chief Reynolds held up his hand. "That's enough. Don't get so carried away. Los Angeles is full of weirdos who burn candles and chant to the moon. If they arrested everyone who thinks he's got some kind of pipeline to super power, there wouldn't be standing room in the city jail. Now I will explain about you three to the Los Angeles police, and that won't be easy. But please do me a favor. Keep out of other people's houses, or you'll really collect a load of buckshot some day."

When he had gone, Pete said, "You should have told him about Miss Osborne and that necklace."

"I couldn't," said Jupiter. "Allie is our client and we have to protect her. And Miss Osborne would deny our story, anyway."

In the office of the salvage yard, the telephone rang. Jupiter went to answer it. He was back outside in seconds. "That was Allie," he said. "The power of the singing serpent has been invoked against her aunt! The cobra was just delivered!"

Living Terror

18

Allie was waiting in the doorway when the boys arrived at the Jamison house. She had the cobra in her hands. It was not a piece of jewelry, like the serpent which Margaret Compton had received. It was a gilt statue about six inches tall. The body of the snake was a heap of shining coils. The hooded head reared out of this. Red eyes sparkled as Allie held the thing up.

"Who was the messenger?" asked Jupiter Jones.

Allie led the way to the living room and put the statue down on the coffee table. "I don't know," she said. "Someone rang the bell and left the box on the front porch and took off."

"I don't suppose it matters," said Pete.

"No, I don't think it does. What does matter is that Aunt Pat got to the box before I did. Even before she unwrapped it, she was shaking. She knew."

"And then?" asked Bob.

"She saw the snake and she read the card."

Jupe bent over the white square of cardboard on the table. " 'Belial will claim his own. A soul is more precious than diamonds,' " he read aloud.

"They printed it nice and big, so she'd be sure to get the message," said Allie.

"And she got the message?" said Bob.

"Well, she fainted. I never saw anybody faint before. I didn't know what to do. After a while she opened her eyes and began to moan. I got her upstairs and put her to bed."

"Will she talk with the police now?" asked Bob.

"No. I told her she had to. I told her we had real evidence—the wrappings and the card and all. She said it wouldn't do any good. She said it might be too late, and the only thing that might help would be to give Shaitan the real necklace."

Jupiter started. "She isn't going to do that?"

"She can't," Allie told him. "She hasn't got it. I found it."

The Three Investigators looked at her, waiting.

"We saw a movie on TV a while back," Allie explained. "It was a spy picture, and the lady spy hid some microfilm in a box of bath powder. Aunt Pat doesn't have a lot of real original ideas. After you left this morning, I went into her bathroom and there it was in the powder box."

"I hope you found a good place to hide it," said Pete.

"In case I get run over by a bulldozer before my folks come home, look in the oat bin in the garage," Allie told him.

"Not bad," said Pete.

"No. Except that now I'm the one who's got to decide, and it's rough. Aunt Pat just lies there in bed and looks at the wall. I'm afraid she's really sick. I mean really, truly sick."

"She may get worse," warned Jupe. "She hasn't been well for some time, has she?"

"No. Not since Mrs. Compton's accident."

"I don't think you should be alone with her," said Jupe.

"I'll call Aunt Mathilda and ask her to come and help you."

Allie brightened suddenly. "Jupe, your aunt's a strong character, isn't she? Do you think if we told her the whole story, she could make Aunt Pat talk?"

"Aunt Mathilda is made of iron," said Jupe, "but in this case, I don't think she could help. Your aunt is too terrified of Shaitan and Ariel. No, it will be better if we just tell Aunt Mathilda that your aunt is having an attack of nerves and you can't handle it alone."

"I can't," said Allie.

"Okay," said Jupe, and he went to the telephone and called the Jones house. Within fifteen minutes Aunt Mathilda was in the house. She surveyed the situation, frowned fiercely at the sight of Pat Osborne huddled in her bed, decided that Allie needed a nap and that the boys would have to leave.

"You and your uncle can eat dinner out," she told Jupiter. "I'll stay here tonight and we'll see how things are in the morning." Aunt Mathilda then disappeared into the kitchen to explore the Jamison refrigerator and the cupboards. Jupe heard a pot clang down on the stove.

"You'll have a good meal tonight," he told Allie.

"I don't like to leave," said Pete. "I mean, shouldn't we go on guard duty here to make sure nothing else happens?"

"Disaster has already struck," said Jupiter. "I don't think anyone will try anything more now. Besides, Aunt Mathilda will cope, and she isn't afraid of singing serpents or anything else that I know of."

He turned to Allie. "Even if your aunt won't talk," he said, "you can. You can call the police. You said yourself, you have to decide."

Allie shook her head. "It would be a nightmare. What

could I say? That my aunt's being victimized by witches? And she's so ashamed. She thinks she's the one who hurt Margaret Compton."

The kitchen door opened. "Jupiter!" said Aunt Mathilda sharply. "Pete! Bob! You boys go on now and let that child get some rest."

The boys went, and when Jupe called the Jamison house late that evening it was a snappish Aunt Mathilda who answered the telephone. She told Jupe that Allie was sleeping and that Pat Osborne was not, and that she had the situation well in hand. She then told Jupe to go to bed and not to call again.

Jupe went to bed and lay for a long time staring at the ceiling. He finally slept, and dreamed dark dreams in which he followed a flickering candle down damp and moldy corridors while unseen things slithered at his heels. He woke in the silent hour before dawn and thought of the little serpent on the table in the Jamison living room. He thought of Pat Osborne, wasted and sickened by fear.

In his mind's eye, Jupe saw Shaitan again, with his dark cloak and his ghastly, pallid face. Two nights before, Shaitan had lounged amid his seedy black trappings and plotted leisurely plots. Now the man was in a hurry. He had come openly to the Jamison house to threaten Pat Osborne. Why?

Jupiter decided that he knew why. In the blaze of floodlights at Torrente Canyon, Shaitan and his accomplice had seen Jupiter Jones—a curious boy snooping on unusual householders. But Shaitan must also have seen the man with the mustache, Bentley. And Bentley had acted quickly to save Jupe and to defy Shaitan. In some way, Bentley had frightened Shaitan.

Jupe twisted and turned in his bed. If only he could find Bentley. But there seemed no way. The mysterious houseman might be the key to the entire affair, but Jupe could think of no strategy that would lure Bentley into the open. Meanwhile, Pat Osborne was growing more and more ill. Was her terror of Shaitan strong enough to kill her? And Hendricks, the unsuspecting owner of a delicatessen on Beverly Boulevard. What would happen to Hendricks?

Then Jupe remembered the book Bob had taken from the library—the book on witchcraft. It had been written by a professor at Ruxton University, and Ruxton was not ten miles from Rocky Beach. Jupiter suddenly smiled. Even without Bentley, he might find a way to help Pat Osborne. And if Shaitan was in a hurry now, so much the better. The Three Investigators had to fight a defensive battle, and before he dropped off again, Jupe knew what the next move would be.

The Serpent Strikes Again

19

The Three Investigators were at the Jamison house bright and early. When they arrived, Aunt Mathilda was going upstairs with a breakfast tray for Pat Osborne, and Allie was in the kitchen gulping orange juice.

"I've decided what to do about the necklace," Allie told the boys. "I'm going to return it to Van Storen and Chatsworth. Let them worry about it."

"Good!" applauded Bob.

"And you?" asked Allie. "What will you be doing?"

"There's a man in Los Angeles named Hendricks," said Jupe. "He owns a delicatessen and we think he will be next to receive the serpent. I believe it will happen quickly—perhaps today. Shaitan wants to finish up his operation. Hendricks is Noxworth's competitor, and Noxworth is due to pay tribute to Belial. We're going to Los Angeles."

"But what about Aunt Pat? She's in awful shape."

"Aunt Mathilda is here," Jupe reminded her. "You can stay. You can send for the man to come from Van Storen and Chatsworth, can't you?"

"Yes, I can. But what if Shaitan shows up?"

"He won't," Jupe predicted. "Allie, your aunt believes in the power of the serpent, and it has made her very ill. Shaitan knows her so he knows this. He won't come here. He'll wait for her to send for him."

"I don't think she can send for him," said Allie. "She can hardly move. She's almost paralyzed."

"There is a way we can help your aunt, Allie, but first we have to think of Hendricks. What we have in mind for Miss Osborne will take time, but she has some time. Hendricks may not."

"What are you going to do?" asked Allie.

"We're going to stake out Hendricks' store," said Bob.

"Then I'm going, too," declared Allie.

"You are not," said Pete. "Shaitan might get rough. That Hendricks is no weakling."

"I am going!" snapped Allie. "Listen, if Aunt Pat has time and Shaitan won't come here, the necklace is safe where it is. I will not sit here and stew while you catch the nuts who've made all this trouble. I'm going!"

Aunt Mathilda came in with the breakfast tray.

"Mrs. Jones, I'm going into Los Angeles," said Allie quickly. "I want to talk to Aunt Pat's doctor. Can Jupiter come with me?"

Aunt Mathilda looked puzzled. "I think you should get her doctor," she said. "Your aunt isn't a bit better this morning and she won't eat a thing. But why can't you telephone? Why go all the way to Los Angeles?"

"I can't remember his name," said Allie, "and the number isn't in Aunt Pat's book. But I do remember where his office is. It's in a building on Wilshire next to a church. It's near Western. Once I get there, I can find him."

"There must be an easier way," said Aunt Mathilda. "Why don't we just ask Miss Osborne?"

"Haven't you noticed?" said Allie. "She won't talk. I asked but she wouldn't tell me."

"All right," said Aunt Mathilda, "but don't dillydally. Jupiter, get Hans to drive you in the truck. It would take all day by bus, and your uncle doesn't have time."

Allie hugged her. "Thanks, Mrs. Jones!"

The boys said nothing. They followed Allie out, leaving Aunt Mathilda to scrape Miss Osborne's untouched breakfast into the disposal.

Hans gladly got out one of the salvage yard trucks for the drive into the city. "Beverly and Third," directed Pete, and he climbed into the back of the truck along with Bob and Jupe. Allie rode in the cab with Hans.

At Beverly and Third, Jupe asked Hans to drive around a corner and park on a side street. Hans did so, then reached across the seat to open the door for Allie. "You want me to come with you?" he asked the boys.

"No," said Jupe. "You wait here and relax. We may be gone for quite a while."

"Okay." Hans took a newspaper from under the seat and prepared to relax.

Allie and the boys rounded the corner and cut across the Hendricks parking lot. "That's Noxworth's store over there," said Pete, pointing to the untidy place across the street.

Allie's nose wrinkled with distaste.

The door of the Hendricks store opened and a small boy scooted out. Hendricks was behind him. "Don't come back today," Hendricks told the child.

Jupiter reached the door just as Hendricks was putting a key into the lock.

"Sorry," said Hendricks. "I'm closed."

"You received the serpent," said Jupiter.

Hendricks straightened up, looked around and saw Pete. "You again!"

"Mr. Hendricks, we want to help," said Pete.

"You do, do you? Okay, the cops filled me in on you. You kids are a bunch of amateur private eyes and you think you're on to some big witch doctor thing. Now I think you're nuts, but I can't chance any lawsuits so I'm closing. Beat it."

"You received the serpent," said Jupe again.

Hendricks reached out and gathered up a fistful of Jupe's shirt. "Did you bring that thing?" he asked. "If you did, I'll wring your neck!"

Jupe didn't try to break away. "We didn't bring the serpent, but we know it must be a cobra with jeweled eyes. How did it arrive?"

Hendricks studied Jupe's face, then let go of his shirt. He opened the door and pointed toward his counter. There was a gilded cobra, a duplicate of the one that had been sent to Pat Osborne.

"I went in the back room for a couple of minutes," said Hendricks. "When I came back, that thing was on the counter."

"I see," said Jupiter.

"So you see. I'm glad. Now go. I've called the cops, but I don't want anyone around just in case something does happen. So blow! Scram!"

A little girl scudded up to the store. Hendricks grabbed her shoulder and spun her around. "Go home to your mother and stay there," he ordered.

She gaped at him.

"Home!" shouted the delicatessen man.

The little girl went.

"Customers!" complained Hendricks. "They're like termites. You can't get rid of them."

A man wearing stained blue trousers and an over-sized, ragged coat made his unsteady way around the corner of the building. "Coffee?" he pleaded.

Allie examined the newcomer with interest. She had seen few panhandlers in her life, and this one was especially seedy. He must not have owned a shirt, for pink, wrinkled skin showed at the neck where his shabby coat was open. His gray hair had gone uncut for many a month, and the stubble on his cheeks was days old.

"Coffee?" he said again. "Say, mister, maybe a sandwich? I haven't eaten for two days."

Hendricks dug into his pocket and pulled out a roll of bills. He peeled off one without even looking at it and thrust it at the tramp. "I'm closed. The guy across the street will sell you a sandwich."

"You're a good man," said the tramp warmly. He took the money, turned, stumbled and fell into the rack of newspapers that stood beside the shop door.

"Blast!" cried Hendricks.

The tramp thrashed about, a jumble of arms, legs and newsprint. "S'okay!" he said. He untangled himself, lurched to his feet and ambled away.

"Hey, mister!" called Allie. "Wait a second!" She darted forward to pick up a small, square black object from amid the drift of papers that now blocked Hendricks' entrance. "You dropped your radio."

The tramp began to run.

"Allie." Jupe kept his voice very calm. "Allie, give that to me."

"Good lord!" said Hendricks.

Allie looked at the little black box in her hand. "What is it? What's the matter?"

Hendricks snatched the thing and threw it. He threw blindly. It arched high in the air, landed on the sidewalk across the street, bounced twice and hit the wall of Noxworth's little market.

There was a flash and a roar, and the windows of Noxworth's Mini Market collapsed inward!

Jupe had a glimpse of Noxworth's face, white with terror, peering from behind a counter. Then Hendricks was racing down the street after the fleeing tramp.

"It was a bomb!" said Allie. "I thought it was a radio."

"Allie, my girl, you've led a sheltered life," declared Pete. "Hardly any real tramps own transistor radios."

Wanted: One Witch Doctor

20

On the return trip from Los Angeles, Allie sat in the back of the truck with the boys.

"Now the police will question Aunt Pat, won't they?" she asked.

"I'm sure they'll be gentle with her," said Jupe. "After all, she isn't a criminal."

"I wanted to keep her out of this."

"There wasn't any way," Bob told her. "Once the police knew how dangerous Shaitan was, we had to tell them everything."

"Allie, you were great," said Pete. "If you hadn't picked up that bomb, Hendricks' store would have been blown up." He chuckled. "I'd hate to see anything happen to Hendricks. What a guy! How'd you like the flying tackle when he caught up with that bogus tramp? And the way he sat on the crook until the cops got there?"

"I enjoyed the look on Noxworth's face more," said Jupe. "The last thing he expected was to have *his* windows blown in."

The truck stopped in front of Allie's house. Aunt Mathilda must have been watching for them, because the front door opened immediately.

"Where have you been?" called Aunt Mathilda. "Miss Osborne is much worse. Dr. Peters is with her now. I had to call him. Did you find her own doctor?"

"No, we didn't." Jupe hurried up the walk. He looked past Aunt Mathilda and saw Dr. Peters.

"Does she have any close relations here?" asked the doctor.

Allie skidded past Jupe and Aunt Mathilda. "I'm it, at the moment," she said.

"I want to move her to a hospital," Dr. Peters said. "She won't consent."

Allie went up the stairs two at a time. Jupe followed her.

Miss Patricia Osborne looked like a shrunken doll under the covers of her big tester bed. She turned away when Allie came into the room.

"Aunt Pat, you've got to snap out of this," scolded Allie. "It's all over. Shaitan is a con man and the cops are going to grab him."

Pat Osborne didn't stir.

Allie seized her arm and shook her. "You've got to help yourself now. Come on! You need to be in the hospital."

Miss Osborne touched Allie's hand. "The necklace," she whispered. "Get it, Allie, please?"

Allie pulled away. "No. You can't give the necklace to Shaitan. Didn't you hear what I've been telling you? By this time, Shaitan's in jail where he can't hurt anyone."

"You betrayed him?" Fresh horror showed in Pat Osborne's face. "Allie, he'll blame me!"

"Nonsense!" Allie tugged at one of her wrists. "Come on, now, Aunt Pat."

Jupe took Allie's elbow. "Let her alone," he counseled.

He led Allie into the hall. "She can't help herself," he said. "Don't you see? She's more afraid of Shaitan in jail than out. There's only one thing to do. We fight fire with fire."

"How?" asked Allie.

"She's been bewitched."

"Jupiter Jones, you know that's hogwash!"

"But your aunt believes it, and it's killing her. We have to take off the curse. We have to find another witch doctor. It's in all the anthropology books. When someone's been cursed, you find another witch doctor to send back the curse."

Allie sagged against the wall. "Where do we get a witch doctor?"

"I think I know." Jupiter started downstairs.

In the lower hall, Bob and Pete milled around a worried Aunt Mathilda. The doctor was pacing in the living room.

"That professor at Ruxton University," said Jupe to Bob. "The one who wrote the book on magic. Do you remember his name?"

"Bannister, I think. No. No, it's Barrister. Henry Barrister."

"That sounds right. And Ruxton is just over the hills in the valley." Jupe started for the kitchen, and the two other boys trailed him.

"Are you going to do what I think you're going to do?" asked Bob.

"I am," said Jupe. "We've had black magic, and now we need a white witch. It could be Barrister. He certainly knows the subject."

Jupe took the telephone from the wall and dialed the information operator. "Have you a listing for Henry Barrister in Ruxton?" he asked.

Bob put a pad on the counter in front of Jupe and handed him a pencil. Jupe wrote down a number the operator gave him and hung up. "If only he's at home," he said.

He dialed the Ruxton number. At the other end of the line, a telephone rang and rang. Then there was a click as someone lifted the receiver.

"Is this Dr. Barrister of Ruxton University?" asked Jupiter.

After a pause, the other boys heard Jupiter say, "Good! My name is Jupiter Jones, Dr. Barrister, and I need your help. It's difficult to explain over the telephone, but there's a woman here who has had a curse put on her, and we—"

Jupiter stopped talking and listened.

"Yes, she's very ill," he said.

Again Jupiter listened.

"Yesterday," he said. "A package was delivered to her. It contained a statue of a serpent."

After a few moments, Jupiter said, "I'm calling from Rocky Beach. The woman's name is Miss Patricia Osborne."

There was another pause, and Jupe said, "That's very kind of you." He gave the address of the Jamison house and hung up.

"He's coming," he told Pete and Bob. "He said he'll bring someone who can take off the curse."

"Hot dog!" crowed Pete. "A voodoo priest, maybe?"

"We'll see," said Jupiter.

The kitchen door opened and Aunt Mathilda put her head in. "Jupiter, what are you doing?"

"I found a doctor, Aunt Mathilda. Dr. Barrister."

"Thank heavens! Dr. Peters isn't able to get anywhere with Miss Osborne. Maybe she'll listen to her own doctor."

"Let's hope so. He's on his way."

"Good. I'll go and sit with her in the meantime. And one of you boys should see to that horse."

Allie drifted into the kitchen. "I'll take care of Queenie," she told Aunt Mathilda.

"The doctor's coming," said Jupe to Allie.

"You found one? That's great!"

Aunt Mathilda went upstairs and Dr. Peters took his leave, fussing and promising to return later. The boys wandered out to the veranda and sat down on the steps. Allie joined them presently. "How long will it be?" she asked.

"Very soon now," said Jupe.

And very soon a car turned onto the street and came at a rapid clip toward the Jamison house. It swerved into the driveway and the motor died. The driver got out and rushed up the walk.

"Jupiter Jones!" said the man.

Jupe started, and so did the others.

"Miss Jamison, I'm very sorry," said the man to Allie. "I had no idea things would go so far."

Jupe stood up. "Just who are you?" he demanded.

"I'm Dr. Barrister, and I should have known better. I thought they were the usual harmless dabblers in magic."

Allie gasped. "You . . . you shaved off your mustache!" she managed at last.

The man who had been known as Bentley touched his upper lip and smiled. "It wasn't real. I thought if I was going to be a snoop, I'd need a disguise."

Mara's White Magic

21

Dr. Barrister sat in the Jamison living room and turned the little figure of the cobra in his hands. "An intricate bit of work," he said, "but then, they weren't playing to a primitive audience. A wax doll wouldn't have been convincing."

"Does it matter what the witch uses?" asked Pete.

Barrister put the serpent down. "Not at all, so long as the victim knows he's been cursed. The power of suggestion takes over. The victim is terrified, and the terror doesn't end."

"Can you help?" asked Allie. "Can you make Aunt Pat believe you're taking the curse off?"

"Not I. Do I look like a witch doctor?"

Allie and the boys had to admit that he didn't. Whether you called him Bentley or Barrister, he was the same calm, inoffensive person.

"Your aunt has seen me pushing a vacuum cleaner in this house," he said. "She wouldn't believe in me, but I think she'll believe in Mara. Mara is very convincing. She's waiting in the car. I've explained the entire affair to her and she knows what to do."

"Is she a witch doctor?" asked Bob.

"She's a gypsy, and she does seem to have certain gifts," said Barrister. "She can cure warts, for example, and she has had some success as a fortune teller. She's also mastered a ritual which is guaranteed to send the most stubborn curse back to the one who inflicted it. You'll have to help her, but you may enjoy that. I'll go get her."

He went out of the room and returned shortly, bringing with him a wrinkled woman whose hair was bound up with a number of scarfs. Mara's blouse was a faded pink, and her wide green skirt reached to the tops of her scuffed shoes. There was an air about her of dust and old clothing, but there was also a brightness. Her black eyes sparkled under shaggy brows.

She picked up the serpent. "Is this it?"

"That's it," said Dr. Barrister.

"Hah!" said Mara. The gypsy nodded to Allie and the boys. "We will work together," she told them. "You do what I say and you say nothing. Do you understand?"

"We understand," said Jupe.

"Is the woman upstairs?"

"Yes," said Allie.

"Then we will go." Mara made for the stairs, carrying the serpent.

"Merciful gracious to heavens!" At the foot of the stairs, Aunt Mathilda came face to face with Mara and seemed about to go into shock.

"It's all right, Aunt Mathilda," Jupe assured her. "Why don't you wait with Dr. Barrister?"

"Dr. Barrister? Is Miss Osborne's doctor here? Why didn't you call me? What are you up to?"

"Dr. Barrister will explain." Jupiter turned to the professor. "This is my aunt, Mrs. Jones. She's been taking care of

Miss Osborne."

"Delighted to meet you, Mrs. Jones," said Barrister. "Come and sit down and I'll explain. You won't believe me, but I'll explain it all."

Aunt Mathilda stood firm. "Jupiter," she said, "I want you to tell me here and now—"

"Woman, you are in my way!" said Mara.

"What?" cried Aunt Mathilda.

"I have important work to do," said Mara. "If you stand in my way, you will regret it."

The gypsy's bold eyes locked into Aunt Mathilda's stern gaze. For a few seconds, Aunt Mathilda glared at Mara. Then, to Jupe's amazement, his aunt stepped aside. Mara did have gifts.

The gypsy went up the stairs and let Allie lead her to Pat Osborne's room. The Three Investigators followed after.

Pat Osborne did not see Mara until the gypsy stood at the foot of the bed and called out.

"Oh, cursed one!" cried Mara. "Listen to me so you may live!"

Under the covers, Pat Osborne shuddered.

"More pillows," said Mara to Allie. "Put pillows under her head so she may see."

Allie scooted out and got three pillows. She coaxed her aunt to a half-sitting position and propped her up with the pillows.

"Look!" Mara held up the golden cobra. "This is the bringer of evil!"

Pat Osborne winced. "Belial!" she whispered. "The serpent is the messenger of Belial!"

"Hah!" said the gypsy. "Ten spirits I have, each more powerful than Belial. But he who summoned Belial will feel the curse."

The gypsy came around the bed and thrust the shining

cobra toward Pat Osborne. "You must take this into your hands."

"No! No, I can't."

"You must hold it, woman," ordered Mara. She took Aunt Pat's hand in her own and closed the trembling fingers around the snake. "Hold it firm if you would save yourself!"

For the first time, a spark of hope seemed to liven Pat Osborne. She grasped the serpent.

From some fold in her wide skirt, Mara took a green cloth sack. "Green is the color of spring," she told Aunt Pat. "It is the color of life. You will put the evil thing into this green sack."

Without taking her eyes from Mara's face, Aunt Pat did as she was told.

"Good." Mara pulled the drawstrings at the top of the sack, closing the snake inside.

"Lock the door," she said to Allie. "Then light a candle."

There was no shortage of candles in the room. They stood about on every surface—green ones and purple, red ones and white. "A red candle," said Mara. "Red has power."

Allie lit a red candle.

"Now, no one may speak," said Mara.

No one did. No one but Mara herself, and when she spoke it was in a high, reedy voice, in a language that none of them understood. She held the green bag containing the little cobra. She addressed it, chanting and crooning. Sometimes her words were a gentle lullaby, sometimes a harsh and terrible threat.

Suddenly the gypsy clutched the green sack close to her faded blouse, threw back her head, let her eyes roll wildly and fell to the floor.

Aunt Pat stared. Mara's mouth was open, and from her throat came a dreadful, gurgling sound, and then a series of high, keening notes.

Mara the gypsy was singing, and she was singing the song of the serpent.

As the frightful sound went on, Mara twitched. Her back arched so that she touched the floor only with her head and her heels. Then she began to roll, thrashing from one side to another, cradling the sack in her arms, her open eyes sightless.

The scarfs which bound her head came undone, one after another. They slipped away and long, gray hair streamed over her face.

Still the song went on, louder and louder, higher and higher, piercing, chilling.

Pat Osborne sat up straight in the bed.

Mara gave a mighty shudder. She screamed, and her body went limp.

Allie and the boys waited. Pat Osborne watched. The gypsy woman seemed to sleep.

"Jupiter!" Aunt Mathilda's voice was loud in the hall outside. "Jupiter, what's going on in there? Open this door!"

Mara moaned and sat up. She groped at the green sack which somehow had remained in her grasp. She smiled. "I saw him," she said. "There is a man in black. His face is very white. He struggles. He is in the coils of the serpent."

"Jupiter, open the door this minute!" called Aunt Mathilda.

Mara got up from the floor. She went to Pat Osborne with the sack. "It is as I promised."

Miss Osborne's shaking hands tore at the drawstrings that closed the sack. She peered inside, felt the sack, shook it. It was empty.

"My spirits are strong," said Mara. "The serpent has returned to sting the one who sent it. The power of Belial has been broken, and Belial has turned on his master. You have nothing to fear."

She went to the door and opened it. "You can come in," she told Aunt Mathilda. "The woman in bed—she is well again."

The Last of the Snakes

22

"It's like a miracle," Allie told The Three Investigators. "Aunt Pat had soup last night and milk and crackers at bedtime and two eggs this morning. Now she's hungry again."

Allie took two slices of toast from the toaster and began to spread them with butter. "I don't know what I would have done without your Aunt Mathilda," she said to Jupe.

"She's always there when you need her," Jupe informed her. "However, by this morning she has convinced herself that the entire affair of the singing serpent never happened. No matter how Dr. Barrister explained it, she can't believe it. She is now down at the salvage yard, attending to business as usual and seeing that Hans and Konrad are not idle."

Allie put the toast on a tray and poured a glass of milk. "How come you're not at the salvage yard?" she asked. "I had an idea your aunt liked to keep you busy, too."

"Chief Reynolds came to the salvage yard this morning," said Jupe. "The Los Angeles police want to see us again. We're just on our way in."

"Did the Chief have any news?" asked Allie.

"That phony tramp named Ellis is in jail, of course," said Bob.

"That's the place for a bomber," said Allie.

"Chief Reynolds said he talked his head off," Pete told Allie. "Noxworth talked, too. The police collected Hugo Ariel and the man called Max. They were at Torrente Canyon. Noxworth didn't know they'd paid Ellis to bomb Hendricks' store. He only thought something would happen to lay Hendricks low."

"That accounts for everybody," said Allie. "All except one."

"Dr. Shaitan," said Jupiter.

Allie sat down at the table. "They didn't get Shaitan?"

"He wasn't at Torrente Canyon," said Jupe. "He disappeared, leaving everything behind, including his car. Chief Reynolds thinks he's probably in Canada by now."

Allie tucked her feet up on the rungs of her chair. "And what do you think?" she asked.

"You're still our client," said Jupiter Jones. "We can't consider the case closed until Shaitan is safely in custody."

"You'll have a long, long wait," said a voice from the doorway.

Allie spun about in the chair. The boys froze where they were.

The man called Shaitan stood facing them, his back to the hall. He looked very much as he had the night they witnessed the ritual in the black-draped room. However, his cloak was streaked with dust and matted with burrs. In one slender hand there was a gun.

"I've gotten awfully careless about locking the doors," said Allie bitterly. "Anyone could wander in here."

"Many people have wandered in in the past day," said

Shaitan. "They're all gone now, aren't they? All except you brats and that fool of a woman."

"You're very well informed," said Jupiter Jones. "Have you been watching the house from the hill beyond the meadow?"

The man bowed to Jupe. "It was tiring," he said. "It was also tiring to walk the mountain trails to Rocky Beach. However, I decided it would be safer to abandon my car when I saw the police drive up to my front gate."

"Just for curiosity's sake, how'd you get out of that house on Torrente Canyon?" asked Pete. "The police got Ariel and Max."

"Fortunately, I was in the back garden when they came."

"So you went over the wall and left your buddies to take the rap," said Bob.

"Who wouldn't?" snapped Shaitan. "Now that stupid woman is upstairs, I suppose." He gestured with the gun. "You four will go up ahead of me. When I've had my little talk with Miss Osborne, I'll make sure that no one leaves this house for some time."

"You will not see my aunt," said Allie evenly.

"Allie, he's got a gun!" warned Pete.

"I don't care. He's done enough. He's not going to see her!"

Very deliberately, she put her hands on her hips and looked straight into Shaitan's weary face. "I know what you want," she said. "You want the Empress Eugénie necklace. Well, it isn't here and Aunt Pat doesn't know where it is, so get lost. You've had all you're going to get."

"If it's in a bank or at the jewelers', it can be retrieved," said Shaitan calmly. "Miss Osborne will telephone. And if it's hidden here, it can be found."

"It isn't in a—"

"Allie!" cried Jupe.

Shaitan's eyes went from Allie to Jupe, then back to Allie.

"You were going to say it isn't in a bank," he said. "Is it at the jewelers'? No. Somehow I think it isn't at the jewelers'. And not in this house? Now where would one hide a priceless necklace like that?" He waved the boys back and came close to Allie. "You know. You'll tell me."

Allie drew back. "I don't know."

"Of course you know. You know all the places it isn't, so you know the place where it is." His right hand still held the gun, but his left hand flashed out. His fingers closed on Allie's shoulder. "Where is it?"

"Take your hands off her!" yelled Pete.

"I won't tell," shouted Allie. "You can go jump!"

"You'll tell." The hand tightened on Allie's shoulder and Shaitan began to shake the girl.

"Stop that!" yelled Bob.

Out beyond the back court, Allie's Appaloosa mare stomped in her stall. Her excited whicker came clearly to them.

"What's that?" demanded Shaitan.

"Only Queenie," said Allie. "My mare."

"Oh, the Appaloosa," said Shaitan. "Yes, I know about her. You care a great deal about that horse and she . . . she has a stall in the garage."

No one spoke.

"Not in the house," said Shaitan. "In the garage. Yes, the necklace is hidden in the garage, where no one can get to it without disturbing the horse. That's what you did, isn't it?"

Allie pulled away from him.

"Out, all of you!" ordered Shaitan.

The horse whinnied again.

"Go on!" commanded Shaitan. "Out to that garage and show me the necklace!"

"I won't!" Allie was almost in tears.

"Do as he says, Allie," said Jupe. "You're not bullet-proof."

"He won't get far," Bob predicted.

"We'll see about that," said Shaitan. He herded them out the back door and across the court. The garage door stood partly open. Jupe swung it wide and they went in.

"Now where is it?" demanded Shaitan.

Queenie bobbed her big head up and down and whin-nied at the sight of Allie.

Shaitan looked at the horse. "You wouldn't hide it in the stall," he decided. "It might get stepped on or eaten. Let me see. The hay? Perhaps. Or the oat bin?"

Allie stiffened ever so slightly.

"It's the oat bin!" cried Shaitan. "You put it in the oat bin!"

He curtly ordered the boys to stand next to the stall. He then shoved Allie toward the feed bin. "Get it!" he said. His voice was very cold. "Get your hands in that thing and dig out the necklace or I'll break your arm."

Cautiously, without looking around at the horse, Pete undid the latch on Queenie's stall.

"Get it!" said Shaitan again. He grabbed Allie's wrist and twisted her arm behind her back.

"You're hurting me!" cried Allie.

Pete stepped to one side and looked at the Appaloosa. The mare's ears were flat against her head.

"Go, Queenie!" shouted Pete, and he swung open the door of the stall.

Queenie moved like a dappled fury. Her hoofs beat briefly on the cement floor of the garage, and then she reared over Shaitan, flailing at the air and screaming as only a furious or terrified horse can scream.

Shaitan let go of Allie. "Get away!" he yelled. His gun swung to take aim at the horse.

"No!" Allie struck at his arm.

The gun went off. The sound of the shot seemed to fill the garage almost to bursting, yet the boys distinctly heard the bullet whine off the floor and splatter into the wall.

Queenie's hoofs struck the pavement. Her big head lunged forward. Her big mouth opened and her teeth clamped down on Shaitan's arm.

Shaitan screamed and dropped the gun. It skidded across the cement. Jupe crouched without taking his eyes from Shaitan, who was trying to pull away from the horse. He picked up the gun.

"It's all right, Allie!" shouted Jupe. "Get the mare away."

Allie ran and threw her arms around Queenie's neck. "Easy, girl," she said. "Let go! Easy!"

The Appaloosa released Shaitan, and the sinister high priest sagged back into a corner of the garage, holding his injured arm close to his body.

Jupe put himself between Shaitan and the door. "Don't try to leave," he said quietly. "I'm not an excellent shot and I might do you some serious damage without intending it."

Shaitan saw the gun in Jupe's hand. He said nothing. He sat there, holding his arm, panting.

Bob stepped behind Jupe. "I'll call Chief Reynolds," he said. "It won't take him five minutes to get here."

"No hurry," said Jupiter Jones cheerfully.

Pete grinned at Queenie. Allie was coaxing the mare back into her stall. "I always had an idea that animal might bite," declared Pete. "Only I never expected it would come in so handy."

Mr. Hitchcock
Asks Some Questions

23

"I sent for you," said Alfred Hitchcock, "because my curiosity is aroused."

The famous motion-picture director tapped a heap of newspapers which were on his desk and looked searchingly at The Three Investigators. "I read of a bombing in Los Angeles. The crime was witnessed by three boys from Rocky Beach, and by a girl about your age. The names of the minors were not published."

Bob handed a file across the desk to Mr. Hitchcock. "We were there," he said.

"On a case, eh?" said Mr. Hitchcock. "I had an idea that might be it." He opened the file and read Bob's notes on the Mystery of the Singing Serpent.

It was quiet in the office then, except for the rustle of papers. Finally Mr. Hitchcock looked up from the file. "It's not complete."

"I'm still working on it," said Bob.

Mr. Hitchcock sniffed. "Astounding what people will believe," he said. "I suppose the cobra you saw at that house in Torrente Canyon was some sort of special effect?"

"They had projectors in the ceiling to throw images of the serpent on the column of smoke," said Pete. "You'd think it wouldn't work. You'd think they'd need special glasses to convince people they were seeing a real snake, but with all that movement in the smoke, it did work. It looked like a real, live, three-dimensional snake."

"Even we were fooled," said Jupiter, "and those people wanted to believe in the serpent. Of course, the serpent *had* to sing. They had to cover up the noise from the projectors."

"There's usually a reason for everything," said Mr. Hitchcock. "How did the serpent sing?"

"It was Ariel," said Jupe. "We thought he made the noise with some device. He didn't. He used to be a ventriloquist, and he could make that noise without showing any strain whatever. With Mara, we could see who the singer was."

"Mara has talents, doesn't she?"

"Many," admitted Jupe. "She's a quick mimic. Dr. Barrister played his tape of that session in Allie's dining room as they were driving to Rocky Beach. She could sing like a serpent before they ever turned in the drive.

"Mara also did something clever with the green sack in which Miss Osborne placed the serpent statue. She won't admit it, but Dr. Barrister is sure she had a second sack hidden in her skirt. She switched sacks while she was rolling around on the floor, gave the empty sack to Miss Osborne and walked off with the serpent."

"That's a very old trick," said Mr. Hitchcock. "Has Dr. Barrister told you why he was so interested in Miss Osborne and the fellowship?"

"He's writing a book on the psychology of superstition," said Jupiter Jones. "He knows most of the strange cults that exist in Los Angeles because that's his subject. He's even joined many of them. And Miss Osborne had joined many of them. He'd seen her often—many times before he became Bentley the houseman. Then she dropped out of all of them. She and Madelyn Enderby."

"This intrigued him?" asked Mr. Hitchcock.

"Yes, because it didn't seem in character. Miss Osborne was obviously looking for something special in these strange groups, and so was the Enderby woman. He wondered if they'd found it somewhere else, so he asked his wife to have her hair done at Miss Enderby's shop. Fortunately, Madelyn Enderby likes to talk, and she talked a great deal about the fellowship. Dr. Barrister got actual names and places. He checked on the members and discovered that all of them were people of means."

"He was suspicious?" asked Mr. Hitchcock.

"Not at first. He thought they were merely a group of well-off individuals who were probably paying good money to sit in that house in the canyon and listen to a serpent sing. This isn't so odd. But he himself couldn't get into that house. Membership was by invitation only, and no one invited him—or his wife. Shaitan probably checked on him and decided he was dangerous.

"So Dr. Barrister took to watching, and when Hugo Ariel moved to Rocky Beach, he took to snooping. And he was very much interested in Pat Osborne. She's a marvelous subject for a man who wants to write a book on the psychology of superstition, and she was different from the other members who went to Torrente Canyon in that she did not have a great deal of money. Shaitan, of course, knew about her wealthy relatives."

"Was it Madelyn Enderby who passed along the word that the Jamison maid had left?" asked Mr. Hitchcock.

"Yes, it was. And that's when he got the idea of putting on a walrus mustache and infiltrating the house to observe Miss Osborne. Then Mrs. Compton had her accident and Miss Osborne sent the necklace out and he became uneasy."

"That's when he really started hanging around that house in Torrente Canyon," put in Bob. "He was there when Allie and Pete and I went over that wall. He saw the floodlights and heard the alarm. And he was there, luckily, when Jupe ran out."

"A good man to have on your side," said the director. "Too bad you frightened him out of the Jamison house when you searched his apartment in Santa Monica. But why did he have that apartment? You said he makes his home in Ruxton."

"It was a blind," said Pete. "He wanted a place near Rocky Beach in case anyone checked on him. Also, he said it was peaceful there and he could get a lot of work done. He has four children."

Mr. Hitchcock chuckled. "Part of the disguise, like the mustache," he said.

"He didn't really need it," said Jupe. "I don't think Pat Osborne would have noticed him, mustache or not. He has the kind of face everyone forgets."

"And when you wanted a white witch, you happened to call him," said Mr. Hitchcock.

"It was like a miracle," said Jupe. "We had no explaining to do, and he had a tape of the serpent singing and could coach Mara. The police used his files to contact members of the fellowship and invite them to a line-up."

"You should have been there!" exclaimed Pete. "You should have seen their faces when they saw Shaitan without his cape or his cap. He looked like a lost leprechaun.

His real name's Henry Longstreet, but he's also known as Harry the Dip because he used to be a pickpocket. Ariel started life as Johnny Boye and once got arrested for peddling fake chrome polish in a parking lot. The man called Max is an ex-burglar and Ellis, who did the actual bombing and sabotaged Mrs. Compton's car, has quite a record. He'll do anything for money."

"Allie told her aunt all about it," said Jupe. "It didn't help much. She's sitting on the patio now, wondering how soon she'll be able to go into Hollywood to consult with Mara."

"A hopeless case," said Mr. Hitchcock. "But what did happen to Miss Enderby's landlady?"

"Nothing," said Bob. "She went to Dubuque because her sister invited her. Probably lucky for her, but Miss Enderby thought Belial engineered the trip and no one told her different."

"What about the man who was worried about a high rise going up next to his property?"

"The land wasn't stable enough for a high rise," said Jupe, "and they credited that to Belial."

"One nice thing," said Pete. "That crystal ball that started the trouble? Allie bought it. Her aunt didn't want it, after what had happened, so Allie took it to the hospital to Mrs. Compton."

Mr. Hitchcock nodded. "A nice gesture."

"It was," said Pete. "Allie's okay, I guess, but I think I'll be glad when she goes to boarding school in the fall. We'll get to use Red Gate Rover again—and besides, she's kind of a strain to be around. Like, she can think up lies quicker than anybody I ever met, and she has this thing about getting her own way."

"It appears so," said Mr. Hitchcock, "but there could be compensations. For example, if you treat her nicely, she might let you ride her horse."

"Thanks a lot," said Pete, "but if I have to go by Appaloosa, I'll stay home!"

ALFRED HITCHCOCK
and The Three Investigators Series